THE VETERAN

WALT DODGE

authorHOUSE®

AuthorHouse™
1663 Liberty Drive
Bloomington, IN 47403
www.authorhouse.com
Phone: 1 (800) 839-8640

Published by AuthorHouse 10/22/2019

ISBN: 978-1-5246-7352-9 (sc)
ISBN: 978-1-5246-7353-6 (hc)
ISBN: 978-1-5246-7351-2 (e)

Library of Congress Control Number: 2017903163

PRAISE FOR WALT DODGE'S OTHER BOOKS

HOW TO SURVIVE A HAWAIIAN HONEYMOON

Walt Dodge has done it again. This talented writer has wed (no pun intended) an exotic locale with his unique brand of humor. "Hawaiian Honeymoon" will leave you howling with laughter and begging for more. In a style reminiscent of Dave Barry and Erma Bombeck, Dodge presents a honeymoon where nothing goes right. This book is a delight for anyone who has visited the Islands. For those who have not, it is a cautionary tale. Hawaii is paradise. The place to take your bride. But when a sign says, "DANGER - Toxic Fumes. Don't go near the cauldron." . . . Don't!

Unless there's a convention in town.

LILA GUZMAN, PhD.
Award winning author of "Lorenzo and the Pirate"

—BLOOMING TREE PRESS

THE NICOLI CONSPIRACY

This story of action and adventure packs an enormous amount of material into relatively few pages. Walt Dodge writes in a friendly and accessible manner... Action and adventure are great subjects...and the author's writing style is quite pleasant.

—FORWARD CLARION REVIEW

TIME SOARING

Taking the ecstasy and freedom of flight experienced only by those few Hang Glider pilots in the world, Walt Dodge gives us a view into the heart and soul of the pilot. His writing style is easy and offers humor and suspense achieved only by a handful of modern writers. This work of science fiction should be on the list of everyone who loves to escape.

—HANG GLIDING MAGAZINE

CURTAIN TIME

Only a few writers, such as John Varley and Walt Dodge, have ever successfully combined science fiction and the theatre. Walt takes us on an elevator ride from the dusty backstage, through time, and into an adventure with humor and style. A must read.

—THEATRE MONTHLY

Acknowledgements

I WOULD FIRST LIKE TO thank my wife for putting up with me over the years and helping me realize the true nature of life and love.

For my children, grandchildren, and great-grandchildren, for being the embodiment of that love.

I would also like to acknowledge the Man upstairs for teaching me to learn and understand the nature of forgiveness. Without that ability I would have eaten myself up with bitterness and hate. We take away the power of those that have done wrong to us when we take away the weapon of hatred.

A special word of gratitude to Danny Hahlbohm: An artist whose incredible talent can only come from one source. His generosity allowed me to use his work on the back cover depicting the focal point of the story. I strongly urge everyone to go to his website (inspired-art.com) and read his story. Also, see the rest of his collection. They are all masterpieces and inspirational.

To all the soldiers who have served and sacrificed, some the ultimate sacrifice, that have gone before me and who have yet to answer the call, my undying gratitude for continuing to make this land in which I live free.

To all the soldiers I fought with in Viet Nam, wherever you are, a heartfelt *Thank You*: Mal, Steve, and Mike, in particular.

To Sergeant Miley, (Yes, he actually existed.) my recruiting sergeant that led me down the right path.

To Eddy Bates, the disabled Marine Force Recon vet that helped inspire this writing.

And, of course, to Lila Guzman: My editor, my mentor, and my friend. For all your work, insight, and professionalism.

Lastly, for all Americans that *have* acknowledged and welcomed home the returning vet with love and understanding. Don't stop. A vet is a special breed with much to give and infinite insight into the nature of their fellow man.

Thank you all.

Prologue

February 17, 1969

"Welcome home, men," announced the pilot over the airplane's speaker system. "Welcome to the United States of America. If you look out the windows, you will see the lights of the Pacific Coast and Seattle."

Cheers rose up. The entire passenger compartment was filled with soldiers and they all screamed with jubilation. They were tired, yet happy. No amount of exhaustion could curb the joy everyone felt. The flight attendants had treated them like royalty during their eighteen-hour flight. The alcohol flowed like water down the Mekong River, yet no one got out of control. The stewardesses were in turn treated with courtesy and respect. Many times the soldiers offered to help with their duties, but they were of course told that it was the airline's pleasure to serve the men coming home from war.

Flying in and out of a combat zone on a commercial airliner felt weird, to say the least, but everything about the Viet Nam War was weird. Why should the mode of transportation be any different? The soldiers had just completed their designated tour of duty and were almost home. Each wore their dress uniforms, whether they be Army, Navy, Air force, or Marine.

The rivers of blood they had each experienced washed away the playful competition between the branches. They all joined together as brothers in a common sense of freedom. Some were going to muster out of the military and go back to their civilian lives. Some would continue their enlistment at some post assigned by the Pentagon after a short leave. But, all would have Viet Nam behind them.

"That," announced Eddy as he looked out the window, "is the most beautiful sight these eyes have ever seen, and *'welcome home'*, are the two most beautiful words I've ever heard. There were many times I thought we'd never make it."

"You can say that again," said Steve.

"Maybe," began Mal, "we had a guardian angel watching out for us, and..."

"If we did," broke in Steve, "he didn't do a very good job. I wouldn't wish on anyone what we went through."

"God works in mysterious ways," stated Mal.

"You can't get over being a preacher's son, can you, Mal?" broke in Steve.

"Amen to that," said Mal.

Steve chuckled. "Preacher Man."

"Son of a Preacher Man," Mal corrected. "But after all we've been through, I'm going to spend the rest of my life being as tight with The Man as I can. We made it. And for that, I am eternally grateful. As for the lights, I've never seen so many in my life. What a welcome home."

"It's like they are putting on a special show just for us," interjected Steve.

"Nice thought," said Eddy. "But, I'm sorry. That's not the case. It always looks like that. You just aren't used to seeing cities this big."

Mal nodded. "Y'all got that right. I'm not sure I *want* to see cities that big. There is a thing called *too many people*. Especially when they're Yankees."

As they laughed together the seatbelt sign came on and they buckled in. The tray tables were up and locked and the seatbacks were in their upright position. Gradually the plane descended until the wheels *chirped* on the runway of McChord Air Force Base. As the brakes were applied and the engines put in reverse, another cheer rose up from the two hundred and seventy-eighty soldiers on the *Freedom Flight* Pan Am 707.

Welcome home! Eddy thought to himself. He leaned his head back and closed his eyes.

Home -- to a land that is free. A land that doesn't have rice paddies. A land that doesn't have monsoons. A land that doesn't have people shooting at them every day and night. A land that doesn't have children with bombs attached to their little bodies waiting to blow themselves, and anyone near, apart. A land that doesn't have diseases they don't have names for, let alone cures. A land that doesn't have vicious trees robbing you of body-parts. A land that has showers, flush toilets, and toilet paper. A land called America.

Home.

Ten minutes later, the plane pulled up to its gate. The three of them walked down the stairs and fell on their faces kissing the ground, crying out of gratitude to the powers-that-be for bringing them home. Many of their fellow soldiers did the same. Others, kept in the cargo hold slept that deep slumber from which we never awaken, weren't able to show their happiness for being brought back to America. They would disembark later with the help of an honor guard, but they were home nevertheless. And still more were left back *in country* as prisoners of war, never knowing if they would ever see free skies again. Some, not many thank God, never made it at all.

In the terminal area the three were then transported to SeaTac Airport where they said their farewells. Promising to write, call, and see each other regularly, they got on separate planes going to different parts of the country. Mal to Thibodaux, Louisiana while Steve headed to Rochester, New York.

Eddy's transfer took him to Los Angeles International.

With high hopes of being welcomed as he remembered seeing in the movies, he spent extra time shining himself up for his appearance when he got off of the plane. He was anxious to see his girlfriend Marge, and imagined her rushing into his waiting arms, letting him know he had been missed and loved. He wore his beret in full dress greens, boots polished to a high spit-shine, pants bloused, captain's bars, and completely decked out with all his new medals: Good Conduct, three service medals, Viet Nam Campaign Ribbon, Viet Nam Service Ribbon, Purple Heart, Bronze Star for Valor with an Oak-leaf Cluster, Silver Star, The Distinguished Service Cross, Prisoner of War Medal, Distinguished Service Medal, Meritorious Unit Citation, Congressional Unit Citation, Presidential Unit Citation, Distinguished Service Sash, and the Hangul (Korean Order of Military Merit - only awarded to six non-Korean nationals in history). Being proud of who he was and what he had achieved, although some of it he could have done without, he actually thought he would be treated with gratitude and respect. He'd grown up watching movies of WWII showing the returning veteran being welcomed home as a hero with songs and dances of jubilation. He'd seen the picture of the sailor bending the girl backwards planting a big kiss on her lips.

Well, he wasn't Gene Kelly, and this wasn't WWII. When he stepped off the plane he was saluted by the people he believed in his heart he had been fighting for.

To his surprise homemade signs, declaring that he and all soldiers like him were the enemy, surrounded him: *Make Peace, Not War, Baby Killers, Assassins, We Don't Want You Back, The Blood of the Innocent is on Your Hands.* This was a greeting not expected. In a little under two years, he had become one of the *bad guys.* How could everything have changed in such a relatively short period of time?

After pushing through the signs and the shouting by the Hippies high on their *Flower Power* and a few other substances, Eddy received a gift from an adoring public: a big slimy green *ball of mucus* hit him right in the face, spit by a girl who couldn't have been more than seventeen. This spoiled brat still living off of Mommy and Daddy, who never had to worry or fight a day in her life, was protesting something that was so alien to her, she didn't know what she was talking about and truly didn't have a right to an opinion. She wasn't much older than another girl he remembered *in country* that didn't have the freedom to protest what she considered an injustice. The grateful cheers of his countrymen were shouts of: "Baby Killer! Murderer! You're scum! War Monger! We want peace, not war! You should have been the one to die!"

What happened to his country in the time he had been gone? This was not the land he left, not the land he knew and loved.

"You should have been the one to die?" she had said.

Maybe he should have.

The War

October 21, 2017

Chapter 1

EVEN FORTY-EIGHT YEARS LATER, HIS homecoming still stung. Sitting alone on a park bench in the cold California rain, Eddy mulled over the details. Three questions came to his mind: *What's changed? Who cares about us now? Who even remembers us?* It was late October, and the precipitation soaked his hair, or what little was left of it, before running down his face and dripping off of his nose and chin. His thoughts and mind were so far away he didn't even notice let alone wipe it off.

Eddy's face felt as numb as his heart. Nothing had been able to reach far enough to thaw the icy prison within which his soul had found refuge. He used to dream. He used to wish he could go back in time and change one thing to heal his life. But now, even that small hope had been killed. He tried to start a movement of veterans united to make a difference. But, politics reared its ugly head and the movement went nowhere. He tried to have a zest for life, but that same life had whipped it out of him.

Most true Viet Nam Vets didn't talk about the war to anyone, other than another Combat Vet. Unless you've had the real experience, you *just didn't understand.* You *couldn't understand.*

Eddy knew why this was the case. He thought of the sights, sounds, and smells. Dead bodies, torn apart and rotting in the jungle. The never ending, sense-piercing sounds of a firefight that went on for days and sometimes weeks. Rotting human flesh, giving up a smell like nothing else in the world that could never be forgotten, combined with the all-present aroma of gunpowder, napalm, and composition B (a plastic chemical explosive with the texture of modeling clay used in claymore mines and flexible enough to wrap around trees, bamboo, bridge supports, and pretty much anything you wanted to blowup).

If only the rain could wash away the stink and slime of his life. His thoughts were immersed in the tide of recalling all the hells and heavens of his Viet Nam experience. Questions of the whys and what-fors had mostly stopped years before. Now he just sat and thought his own private thoughts.

His early life hadn't been so bad. He had a relatively normal childhood growing up in Southern California in an average middle class neighborhood. He went to a private elementary school that he and his brother nicknamed *The Prison* where he had received a better than average education, or at least he came away with a better than average intelligence, except for *street wisdom*. They taught him all the necessary subjects: English, math, history, geography, music, and sports. But they left out one very important part of any child's education: How to deal with others, especially those that didn't think the same way, or grew up in the same environment, as you did. This precious learning experience he had to get the hard way.

After elementary school it was on to public school for junior high and high where he went through the normal trauma of puberty while trying to adjust to how the world actually worked. The *Prison* kept all the students from learning and understanding the society in which they lived, especially Eddy and his brother. All the other students were from wealthy families. They were protected and lived according to a set of rules that Eddy would never attain. Society's restrictions and laws didn't seem to apply to them. Money buys a lot of *looking the other way*. Tuitions were paid up-front and parents or butlers driving Mercedes, Jaguars, Rolls Royce, or Cadillacs picked them up at the end of the day.

Eddy came from a less than affluent background. His father had left when he was two weeks old and his mother never remarried. He and his older brother had to take on the household duties at an early age as his mother worked long hours as a telephone operator. Many times she would work split shifts: Put in four hours then come home to prepare dinner just so she could go back to put in another four, and most often, overtime. Cleaning the dishes and the house were left to Eddy and his brother. They shared these tasks every day and every night. Eddy would wash and his brother would dry, then they vacuumed the floors. On weekends they would dust the inside before going outside to do the yard work. Eddy usually ended up mowing the lawns, his brother would edge and rake, then they both would weed.

Don't misunderstand. They had plenty of time for play and other activities. Eddy joined the Boy Scouts and did quite well. He was awarded his Eagle Badge before he was fourteen and loved the outings and camp-outs the organization afforded him.

His school tuition to the Prison was paid on a monthly basis, and he rode his bike or walked to school. They moved every few years and sometimes the distance became considerable. But his mother wanted them to continue with this school until completion, so they had to get up quite early to have enough time to make it. Most of the time they had to ride the public bus system. Living almost fifteen miles from the school riding their bikes wasn't always a viable option. They did it a few times, but that was just for fun.

On the bus, people of other races and ethnicities gave them an exposure to the *outside world* treasured in their minds for the rest of their lives. Many times, the men on the bus heading to the race track in Santa Anita during racing season, would let Eddy and his brother pick the horses. The next day they were given buttons to wear if a horse won. This was cool. They were treated like they were the children of the men and women. They never felt in danger. They were never talked down to. There was no bigotry. There was literally no difference between them, except for age.

Eddy was treated differently at the school, but didn't understand the reasoning behind the treatment until later in life. He just thought it was normal, as he had never known any other way.

People talk about racial, sexual, religious, and ethnic bigotry. There is something called economic bigotry that is just as immoral and wrong.

Especially when it comes from a source that daily pontificates about how much more right their way of thinking is than anyone else's.

Right is right, and wrong is wrong. There is no compromise or argument. And bigotry, in any form, is wrong.

Eddy made it through high school after adjusting to life as it really was. Sometimes this adjustment came at a cost and a few times it came rather brutally. One such example occurred when he was a junior, eleventh grade, and was driving. There existed an element at this particular high school that didn't see life as Eddy had been raised to see it. This element carried the title of *Joe Bads*. They would just as soon slit your throat as look at you. They dressed differently, and acted differently. They defied all authority and lived as though society and its laws just didn't apply to them. It wasn't like the rich, who felt as though they were above the law. This group simply had contempt for anything and anyone not in their circle. Many ended up dead or in prison. They had the carriage of kids who had nothing to lose, and I suppose they didn't. Many came from alcoholic or drug addicted homes where they themselves were abused, physically and mentally. A couple of the students had at least one parent in prison.

One afternoon, one of the *Joe Bads*, standing on the corner across from the school defying the law pertaining to minors smoking was doing just that. He was smoking and looking for trouble. Out of the blue he flipped Eddy off as he drove by with his girlfriend taking her home at the end of the day. Eddy, in return, flipped him back.

The next day the *gentleman* and four of his cronies confronted Eddy. His minions held Eddy as this idiot proceeded to sucker-punch Eddy in the mouth laying his entire cheek open. Eddy had recently received a full set of braces. These were not made of plastic, but the metal kind with sharp edges. He had to cover them with orthodontic wax at first to keep from tearing up the inside of his mouth. Once the mouth got used to the intrusion, the wax could be removed. He had just removed the protective wax a few days before and the tender flesh was vulnerable. The blood flowed as though he'd had an artery severed.

Being taken to the school nurse didn't do a lot of good, as the only function they had was to call the parents and inform them of the situation and ask them to come and get the student. She did put an ice pack on the cut, which helped to slow down the flow of blood.

Eddy's mom wasn't allowed to leave work so the Vice Principal took Eddy to the local hospital emergency room where he eventually got stitched up and sent home. I said *eventually* because there was a little problem with permission. Eddy was raised in a religion that didn't use or believe in doctors. Well, believe in them or not, his mouth and face needed stitching. So, with the authorization given over the phone by his mother, Eddy got his twenty-seven sutures.

This experience wasn't the first time he had gotten scars, nor would it be the last. But it did serve to open his eyes to the reality that there are consequences to every action. Newton's third law applies to more than apples.

By the time he joined the Army, went through basic, AIT, OCS, Ranger-Airborne, Special Forces, and Black Ops training, his eyes were fully opened and alert. If he were to be asked how he saw life, he would respond that it was more to the negative side than the positive. He saw life and man realistically.

Yet, with all that said, he was still somewhat naive. All humans who have not seen the *Dogs of War* are equally naïve. That trait would be ripped out of him during his tour *in country*.

His duty in Nam wasn't as so many are depicted on the television or in movies. He didn't live in nice air-conditioned barracks in Saigon or Pleiku. He didn't get to flirt with the Mama Sans on the streets, or go into a bar for a cold beer at the end of a four-hour shift on the radio.

He didn't teach a class or flirt with girls. He rarely enjoyed a hot meal and equally as rare slept in a bed as comfortable and exotic as an Army cot.

No. Eddy was a field soldier, one of the battle-tested veterans of the war. He saw friends die. Felt the sting of a bullet. Smelled the odor of death. Heard the cries of the wounded during and after their fragile bodies were torn apart by every means possible one human can think of to rend another human. Tasted the blood of a friend that splattered onto his face and into his mouth, just because he was unlucky enough to be close by when the friend got blown apart. Or, as most vets came to believe, *lucky* enough to not be the one disassembled. He saw it all. And, now he remembered it all as he was destined to do for the rest of his life.

In the forty-five years since he returned home, nothing or no one had been able to penetrate the crystal. Many had tried. His mother, when she was alive, brother, girlfriends, friends, and fellow workers at the many jobs he held, each for a short time, each equally failing.

He had been engaged four times and married twice. The marriages ended the same way for the same reason.

He just didn't give a shit.

He didn't care if his wives stayed or left any more than he cared if the raindrops eventually fell from his nose onto his mutilated hand, a gift from the Great Father, Ho Chi Minh, and his minion, Colonel Nguyên.

His left hand was now useless, frozen with the thumb pulled back and bent in at the knuckle. The center two fingers were pointing down and toward the palm as though he was trying to hold a pencil, and the outer two were straight and stiff. The back of the hand was a road map of scars where the skin had been mutilated (maimed and disfigured) before the bones were broken and the tendons severed.

Shirts and pants covered a multitude of scars on his body from many wounds, but his hand? That was the one he constantly saw whenever he lifted his arm.

As usual, it was the hand that got him thinking again.

Thinking back to the war and the futility of it all. Oh, he believed in the call of his country, doing his duty for God, Country, and Mom's apple pie. But life is a stern Headmaster. Some lessons come harder than others.

Chapter 2

EDDY KNEW THE HISTORY OF Viet Nam and how they came to be entrenched in a war that in the eyes of the Vietnamese had gone on for almost five hundred years. He recalled the time when he was performing a particular *special assignment* found himself in a location that was classified; doing a job his government would never admit he was sent to do. As a member of Black Ops, there were *special times* when he was called away from whatever other duty he was performing, whether it be as an Artillery Commander, Battalion Intelligence S-2, or advisor to the ROKs (Republic of Korea military), and given an assignment. Then for the next few weeks or months his orders didn't come from the Department of the Army but from other, less known and acknowledged, departments. If anyone ever asked about his whereabouts, the Army said he was recovering from one disease or another in some obscure hospital.

He was only in the hospital twice during his entire stay *in country*. The first time: with malaria where he spent a memorable month hallucinating at the Army hospital at Cam Ranh Bay. He remembered how much fun a 105-degree body temperature was and the thrill of being immersed into a vat of ice water. You want to know what cold is? That is cold. Remember, temperature perceived on the body is relative to the temperature of the body itself. If, for example, a person touches ice the temperature difference is between 98-degrees, the body's normal temperature, and the 30-degree ice. That is a 68-degree difference. Now, raise that body temperature to 105 and you have a 75-degree difference. If that doesn't seem like much of a difference to you, try it some time. *There's a difference.* It was either that or having your brain boil from the inside out. Great little mosquitoes they have over there.

The second time Eddy found himself in a hospital was a result of the present nostalgia brought on by his omnipresent hand.

He and two other Special Forces Black Ops (Specially trained Green Berets working on a covert operation) were in an area where no American troops were supposed to be, as usual. The orders came directly from Major Wheeler, the Special Forces commander working under the auspices of the CIA. He also happened to be the son of the famous military war hero Major Sheldon Wheeler. His father had received the Distinguished Flying Cross for his actions above and beyond, which ultimately cost him his life. Wheeler Army Airfield next to Schofield Barracks in Hawaii was named after him.

"Captain Chapman reporting as ordered, Sir."

"At ease, Eddy," replied Wheeler returning the salute. "Take a load off."

Eddy sat as the Major walked around his desk and started to pace. He did this a lot when something bothered him.

"I don't know what kind of idiots think this stuff up but orders are orders," the Major began. "As with all orders of this kind, you retain the right to decline the assignment. Personally, I would suggest it, but the choice is yours."

"The decision has already been made," responded Eddy. "Thank you anyway, Sir. Please continue."

"Alright, then. You and your team are to go with a squad of Montagnards (Americans pronounced it 'Mountain-yards') to a specific location to take out a North Vietnamese Colonel and capture his advisor, a major from a special unit of the Soviet Union."

Eddy recalled hearing about this guy. Standing 6'6", he looked like the typical Russian bear. He was Eddy's counterpart to the Vietnamese. Sent by his country to do subversive work in a foreign land he probably didn't like any better than Eddy did.

He thought, how alike they actually were. Oh well, it was too late to think about striking up a friendship and going out for a few beers or, in this case, vodkas.

The assignment was pretty straightforward. Eddy had performed the same type of assignment twice before without incident. At least, there was no harm to Eddy and his team. Couldn't really say that for the target personnel. One of them ended as just that, a target -- which of course, was the plan.

"Your team will be choppered in about five klicks across the border by Air America," Wheeler continued. "Then you'll travel by foot to the area where the Colonel and Major are encamped. It's a village in Cambodia that's been taken over and is being used as a headquarters for NVA guerrilla raids into Viet Nam.

"S-2 will fill you in on the details. If it's any help, I think the assignment stinks. Taking out the Colonel is one thing, but sticking around to capture some Russian is idiotic. I said so and got my butt chewed out, so you can save your breath. You were handpicked for this from higher up, probably because of the way you performed in that little Korean episode."

"Major," interrupted Eddy. "That was a moment of insanity. I don't know what possessed me to even think up such an idiotic idea. I don't want any awards and, personally, I wish everybody would just forget it ever happened."

"Well, you're just going to have to live with disappointment. You have an entire ROK Battalion and firebase that won't forget it. In fact, my understanding is you have the entire country of South Korea who won't forget it. You are to receive their highest decoration, and you will accept it with dignity."

"Yes, sir."

"I read the report, but we haven't had time for you to tell me about it directly. I'd like to hear it now."

"Well, sir," Eddy began. "An Intelligence report was received that the North Vietnamese Regulars were planning to launch a human-wave attack against the ROK firebase outside of Kontum. My *brainstorm* was to hide, with a small squad of Korean soldiers, in holes we dug beyond the perimeter of the base up on the side of a hill past where we believed their staging area would be.

"We stayed buried for two days as the NVA moved in and prepared for their attack. They had mounted a division for the assault. Their plan was devious.

"They would use a battalion-size force to assault the firebase knowing the normal procedure used against them by Americans and their allies when an assault takes place. Which is, of course, to send an infantry unit by helicopter behind the attacking battalion, turn on the NVA and squeeze them in the middle.

"But in this case, the attacking force would turn around and attack to their rear. Behind the American infantry would be the NVA division. The orders were to leave none alive. The Vietnamese saw Koreans as traitors. The Koreans, on the other hand, considered the Vietnamese beyond contempt. They still do, for that matter.

"But, to continue. We learned of this plan from a captured NVA reconnaissance officer. How they got such damaging information, I can't say, but they got it nevertheless.

"Because of the severity of the TET Offensive, manpower was stretched thin. Fighting was everywhere, and there were no American Forces to call upon. So I came up with the idiotic idea everyone thought was insane, including me. Suicidal. And in retrospect, everyone was right. But...we did it anyway.

"As the NVA spent the night preceding the planned assault getting drugged up while preparing to die, we emerged from the holes we had been hiding in and, using nothing but K-bars, started killing the commanding officers in the camp.

"We literally crawled into the middle of them and started slitting throats, inserting the knives into eye sockets up to the hilts, and finding that the path into the brain through the ear canal gives very little resistance and causes an immediate result. This had the effect of leaving a path of death. Then, we crawled away.

"By morning, the NVA had no leaders. They didn't know what to do. Unlike the Korean and American armies, the NVA didn't pass down battle plans to the lowest privates. Only the highest officers knew what they were supposed to do. And that particular morning the officers with that specific knowledge were unable to command.

"Not knowing what to do, the NVA battalion began its attack on the firebase with the rest of the division joining them. They ran straight into a prepared and waiting firebase with artillery lowered to fire flechette, Willy Peter, and HP rounds point blank into the onslaught.

"It became a route. No unit choppered in behind them. The devastation was reversed.

"As the remaining parts of the division, without leadership, turned to retreat back into the mountains, they ran into our wall of claymores, Bangalore torpedoes, punji sticks, death falls, and mines that we had spent the morning setting up. Plus, as the few that made it scrambled to the top of the mountain in retreat, I was standing there, stupid as hell. I had been wounded during the previous night's blood bath, but was still there, waiting in defiance like an idiot.

"There were a lot of NVA left. But to see an American, standing in total contradiction to what they had been taught of us, as being cowards and weak, waiting to kill them all, was more than they could comprehend."

"I've heard it said," broke in the Major, "that in the afternoon light in the valley ten klicks north of Kontum, of the sight of three hundred NVA, all with their hands on their heads being led to Chieu Hoi to the Korean commanders, by you.

"I further heard, but I find this hard to believe, you didn't even have a weapon trained on them. You had been wounded severely, and upon arrival back to the firebase, a field surgeon had to do some emergency surgery to save your life.

"The story is that you were simply walking in with them, talking to a couple of the NVA that spoke English as if you and the whole group had been out on an afternoon stroll. Was that an exaggeration, or a statement of fact?"

Finally Eddy spoke. "That bit about the remnants of the Division scrambling up the steep hill seeing me. I wasn't alone. I had one of the Korean soldiers standing next to me. The others had been killed."

"That's it?" Wheeler asked.

"That, and they didn't have their hands on their heads. I didn't see any reason for such a show. We just walked in."

"That, is the exaggeration? There were two of you, instead of you alone...and the placement of their hands?"

"Yeah. Well, like I said. I don't like to talk about it. It was a stupid thing to do. I got all but one of my squad killed."

"How many Koreans were with you to begin with?"

"Five."

"Five?"

"Yes! Five!"

"So. Four Koreans died to save more than three hundred lives, and in process you defeated an entire NVA division?"

"Yeah. I guess so." Eddy just kind of sat there with his head hanging down. Not very much embarrassed him, but this one act did.

"You are crazy, Chapman," the Major repeated.

"Yes, sir. But I still don't like getting medals, especially for doing something stupid. Just because it worked, doesn't make it any less crazy."

"Personally, I agree with you. I think you *are* nuts, but that's what makes you good. Best of luck, and get back -- alive."

Chapter 3

EDDY RARELY RESPONDED. BUT, HE knew when asked a question by a superior officer he had to answer. But when enough was said, that was it. And -- he'd said enough. Wheeler usually did the talking for the both of them and there was nothing more to say. He saluted and left.

S-2 filled him in on the details of the mission. He was briefed on all that was known of the Colonel, and the Major. The Colonel was a known sadist. He had a reputation for brutality, not only toward the enemy but toward his own men as well. The North Vietnamese generals and Party Headquarters in Hanoi knew of his activities and allowed it to happen because of the success he demonstrated. If a few of their own soldiers were beaten or killed, what mattered that? As long as he inflicted casualties on the Americans, then that was all that was important.

The North Vietnamese Regulars were promised two things: A bowl of rice a day and a burial when killed. There was an old story of this North Vietnamese Colonel stepping over the bodies of some soldiers lying on the ground dying, but not dead, being asked if some help couldn't be given to his wounded men. His response was, "They have performed their duty to the Party. They have no further purpose. Let them die."

The Russian Major, on the other hand, was his exact opposite. He was known for his compassion and respect for life. No one in S-2 understood how the two were able to work together. But, none of the American Intelligence sources worked in either the Kremlin or Hanoi, so a great deal of speculation was interjected into the reports.

Unreliable, at best.

At least the weather was cooperating. This time of the year it was hit and miss. It could be sunny one moment and a torrential downpour the next. According to the Meteorology section no rain was anticipated for a few days. Eddy actually came to like it when it rained for a couple of reasons. One, the damn humidity could be tolerated. And two, the rain provided a form of cover for the operation. Even though the Vietnamese were used to it, no human likes to stand out in it. A normal reaction is to seek shelter. Shelter means there is a visual block between the sheltered and the outside, which is where Eddy, and his team would be operating. No rain meant no shelter, so he had to be especially cautious to stay invisible.

The village encampment was located in a river valley. At any other time, it would have been quite beautiful, but war takes the beauty out of everything, even nature. The valley had tall mountains on three sides. They were lush and green with foliage. That's what made this an ideal location for the Vietnamese. An attacking force could come from only one direction. The mountains were steep and treacherous to navigate, at best. No major force could come down them without being detected. The Vietnamese didn't believe they would ever even cross the border. They thought of the Americans as weak fools who abide by a set of morals and rules that no one else follows. Their belief system was that there was only one rule in war: Kill, maim, or mutilate all enemy personnel by any means possible. There is no *humanity* in war. There is no *compassion*. There is no *empathy*.

America's policy was that if you're chasing the enemy and they go across a border to another country, and your government promised that country you wouldn't cross their border, you stop. You let the enemy get away.

Idiotic!

No Vietnamese unit cared about rules, borders, or what we Americans consider morals, for that matter. They fought the war their way. The Special

Forces, SEALs, and Marine Forced Recon were the most successful units in country, because they fought the war the Vietnamese way. That's why those units scared the hell out of the gooks.

The mountains were high and steep. The NVA had listening posts up in the hills incase an attack came from a small force otherwise undetected. But the soldiers manning them had grown lax due to inactivity for so long a period. This base camp existed for over two years; an incredible amount of time for anything to last that wasn't a major city.

The Vietnamese had been fighting somebody since 1545, when civil strife railed Viet Nam, splitting the country for nearly two centuries from the peace established by Le Thanh Tong in 1460. This was followed by the French missionary activity in 1772.

In 1787, Pigneau de Béhaine, a French missionary who had long since given up any similarity to a *Man of God*, enlisted the support of Louis XVI to help a pretender to the throne, Aguyên Anh, gain control. France agreed to send men and matériel in exchange for exclusive commercial privileges, but later reneged, and for a good reason.

1789 saw the start of the French Revolution.

1802 ushered in the reign of Napoléon in France, and Gia Long (Nguyên Anh) became Emperor of Viet Nam, unifying the country.

Back and forth relationship with France existed until 1862 when Tu Duc signed a treaty granting broad religious, economic, and political concessions.

The French foothold was firmly in place.

In 1883, France established a *Protectorate*, and ruled Cochinchina (Viet Nam, Cambodia, Tonkin, Annam) as a colony.

1890 was a special year to the Vietnamese. It was the year of the birth of the father of their country, Ho Chi Minh.

In 1911, Ho left Viet Nam, not to return for thirty years, fighting for independence from without.

At the Peace Conference in Versailles in 1919, Ho tried to petition President Woodrow Wilson for self-determination in Viet Nam.

He was declined.

Not receiving help from America, Ho joined the newly formed French Socialist Party in December of 1920 using the alias Nguyên Ai Quoc.

By 1924, Ho found himself in Moscow, a full-time communist agent.

He returned to Viet Nam in 1941 to begin his struggle for independence from within. To the Vietnamese, war was simply a part of life. They knew no other way.

The fighting began and continued to this moment in which Eddy found himself, being asked to *Score one for our side.*

His team consisted of himself, a sergeant, a radio operator, and five Montagnards. Too many, Eddy had thought, so he declined three. The dust-off would take place at Twelve Hundred Hours five days hence. A *dust-off* is when a helicopter picks you up from a predetermined location.

You can't move quietly with too many people no matter how well trained they are. Eddy normally went out with just himself and Mal, his sergeant, and a radio operator, but they were usually FNGs (fuck'n new guys) and prone to making stupid mistakes. In Viet Nam you only make a stupid mistake once.

Just once!

This kind of operation couldn't afford mistakes. It was too important. So Eddy used Steve, an E-4 specialist who had his shit together, along with Mal. The three had worked together before and he knew he could trust and rely on them. They were friends as much as they were fellow combatants. The Colonel and the Russian Major had been causing havoc with operations up and down their area of the border. Massive hit-and-run missions that caused incredible damage. Supply lines were cut. Ammunition dumps were blown up. Base camps were constantly attacked. They had to be stopped.

In present day, as Eddy thought about this, he compared how alike it was to the basic assignment Martin Sheen had in *Apocalypse Now*. He had always thought that Francis Ford Coppola, or Joseph Conrad, the writer of the original novella, *Heart of Darkness* that the movie was based on, had somehow known about his mission. It didn't end the same, but the basic tasks were so much alike.

A crew from Air America inserted him and his team at the designated coordinates. Since they were hitting the ground in Cambodia, using US Military pilots and choppers was not the best idea. All normal uniforms and insignias were removed and dog-tags were left behind. If they were captured or killed, no connection to an American Force could be proved. They then had a two-day hump over some of the worst mountain terrain in Southeast Asia. But, they had spent their entire tour in the Central

Highlands, so this was just another task in a long list. The progression was hard and slow: Up one muddy, slippery jungle mountain and down another. Just so you could do it again, over and over. They slept tethered to trees so they wouldn't slide down the mountain in their sleep, which wasn't much anyway. They took four-hour shifts on watch and no one was exempt. Eddy was an officer, but in the jungle, rank meant shit. Everyone shared all duties. They never referred to each other by rank. It was Eddy, Mal, and Steve. Each was aware of the respective ranks and they were respected accordingly. But in their normal situations...to call each other by rank was ridiculous. It was never *Captain Chapman*. It was always Eddy, or in some cases, *Asshole*.

As they approached the location of the North Vietnamese base, they slowed the pace and took each step as though it was their last. If any one of the team hit a trip-wire or booby-trap the outcome would be final as well as fatal.

Eddy crept up to the crest of the hill to observe the base and stopped. He had the strangest sensation that something was not right. Had he missed a detail? Had something occurred that he should have noticed, but didn't?

Was this a good day to die?

Many of his friends never made it home. Some died more acceptably than others. He remembered one time in particular when walking along a trail in the Central Highlands, the region in the mountains on the tri-borders where Viet Nam, Laos, and Cambodia meet. It was there that the Ho Chi Minh Trail, the main artery for supplies from North Viet Nam to the South, bends into Viet Nam from the two neighboring countries.

As I said, the American forces were not supposed to go into the other countries, so Charlie freely used the supply route. But there, where the road curved into Viet Nam due to a particularly large mountain, American forces could do something.

Yeah! They could do something, all right! They could get the shit kicked out of them on a regular basis because Command wouldn't let them fight.

As an example of not being allowed to fight, Eddy recalled the standing orders requiring all artillery requested had to be preceded by *first round smoke* before any high explosive rounds could be called in.

Smoke was a type of artillery round consisting of a large hollow shell which ejects smoke out of the back at an altitude of about two hundred feet. If you were lucky, you might hit someone on the head with the empty canister.

The idiotic purpose behind this order was to use smoke to warn civilians in the area that a firefight was about to commence so they could leave before the high explosive rounds impacted, causing injury.

Now, Eddy never confessed to being the smartest person in the world, but somehow he couldn't believe it took a nuclear physicist to figure out that if Charlie was shooting automatic weapons, rockets, hand-grenades, and mortars at them, any civilian stupid enough to stick around would have gotten the hint that a fight was underway. And, it might be more beneficial to their longevity, if they...*GOT THE FUCK OUT OF THERE!!!!!*

Eddy felt that most of the civilians were helping the NVA (North Vietnamese Army) anyway. He never dealt with the Viet Cong (South Vietnamese who sympathized with the North). Most Cong were further South and easier to fight. He only dealt with hard-core highly trained NVA.

You can't win anything defending! Eddy thought remembering the ridiculous way the war was staged.

Of course, at the time, Eddy didn't know that they weren't supposed to win. Just sustain the conflict. If some of our sons and husbands died in the process? Well...? It was an acceptable expenditure for the *cause*. And that *cause* was a purely political and economic one.

The memory made him sick.

He thought of walking that trail, as he had done many times. But this time he stopped suddenly as he saw something ahead, right in the middle of the path. He couldn't make out what it was. It looked like a pile, or stack of something. It was about fifty feet in front of him when first spotted. Since he was *point* (meaning the guy walking in front through the jungle and usually the first to get shot), he instantly called for everyone to hit the dirt.

All of his adrenal glands were pumping overtime as he tore buttons off his shirt to get closer to the ground. His normal constant sweating froze. His glands stopped working and his ass puckered. He aimed his M16 at the object and squeezed off a round.

The whatever-it-was didn't move.

He fired again.

Nothing.

Since an M16 round enters the size of a 22-caliber bullet and exits the size of a 12 gauge, Eddy figured the whatever-it-was was dead. So, he slowly crawled up to it, literally an inch at a time. His combat experiences by then led him to believe that nothing in this place was ever *dead enough*.

As he got closer, his mind's self-protection kept preventing him from accepting the reality, kept him from believing the truth, kept him from comprehending the depraved depths that one man can go to in the treatment of another human being. What he had been taught as a child about man being good and caring, had been washed away. No, *blown* away would be a more accurate description. There is nothing noble about man. He wished there was, but knew in the depths of his soul, there wasn't. And what he was about to see permanently imbedded that fact.

When he finally reached the pile and poked it with the muzzle of his rifle, part of *the thing* slipped off the side.

It was a human hand attached to an arm carefully placed on top of the main part of the pile. The hand and arm were encrusted in dried blood and dirt. The skin was a whitish pale blue-green, the color of rot. It seemed as if the skin itself was alive due to the maggots crawling in and out of the lacerations and around the severed humerus bone and surrounding muscle.

The smell was as indescribable and unforgettable as the garden aroma of burning *honey pots* (a nick-name for the smell created by the burning of the defecation in a latrine with diesel fuel), a smell that carried in the wind for miles and totally destroyed all olfactory senses unlucky enough to be down-wind or within the blast radius of a small nuclear bomb.

The closest he could ever think to describe this stench was like walking up to a very large animal carcass that had been laying in the sun and rain for a couple of weeks and shoving your face into the maggot infested intestines that had burst out from the swollen gut.

Only this was worse.

Slowly Eddy stood up. The pile was about two and a half feet high. Looking down on it, he finally accepted the truth.

Left there, in the middle of the trail where any GI would see it, was a human body. *Stacked* was the name they had for this particular display.

It was a favored gift to the Americans from the grateful Vietnamese that displayed for all their total contempt for life.

The body's four limbs were cut off at the junction to the torso. The head was cut off at the neck. The body was then laid on the ground with the arms and legs crossed on top forming a diamond space with the bent knees and elbows. The head was placed in the center with the soldier's severed penis sticking out of his mouth.

It was left to freak-out the Americans, to demonstrate these people's total lack of feelings for the sanctity of life and respect for humanity. They were, and as Eddy thought still are, a people without honor. There was no honor in this, and the effect it had on the American *grunt* was just the opposite they expected.

Whenever any GI saw this type of display, it filled him with a resolve that the Vietnamese culture could no more conceive of than the American could identify with theirs. This would not be allowed to go on. A people who could do such a thing could not be allowed to exist, at least not without being shown that this was unacceptable.

The American GI's gut reaction was one of unlimited *RETALIATION*. The only problem was; the GI's desires had nothing to do with reality. The protected and ignorant politicians at home ruled the war. The GI had no say what-so-ever.

In addition, the Hippie protestor, waving banners and shouting that we had no business over here, had never seen the likes of this display from the *poor victimized Vietnamese*. If they had, they would have put out their marijuana, laid down their signs, and gone home grateful that a few loyal patriots were trying to rid the world of this kind of scum.

Eddy thought that Americans saw the Sixties as the time of our *loss of innocence* starting with the assassination of President Kennedy. When in truth, only the Viet Nam Vet lost his innocence by having it sucked out of him by the scum of the earth -- Politicians. The Vietnamese were simply products of their environment. Don't blame a mule when it kicks you. If it had known better, it wouldn't have done it. The Politicians knew better.

The problem here was, at this moment, it wasn't just anyone who found this particular stack on the trail. It was Eddy. And Eddy had known this man. He recognized the person this carnage used to be. He had trained and served with him. They had talked of life and family, of love and sex, of jobs and ambitions, of hopes and dreams.

His name was Phil ...and Eddy vomited!

He threw up things he didn't believe possible.

He threw up bile that comes not from the stomach but from the very depth of what makes us men. He threw up all that millions had fought and died for over the millennia since that first creature crawled out of the mire and took its first breath of air. He threw up all societies that strive to create order since the beginning of time. He threw up any culture that could breed beings capable of doing such a thing.

Who could think so little of life and have so little respect for that precious gift, that they could treat it so?

He threw up...God!!!!

War meant killing. Yes! This was an accepted and admitted fact. But this went beyond anything Eddy could ever have conceived in his most horrid nightmares. At that instant, something died inside of him. Any tentative hold on childhood and innocence was smashed out of his young twenty-two year old soul. He ceased being a human.

To preserve what little thread of sanity he still retained, he became an animal, the primordial beast that knows nothing but survival.

He thought, *Better he, than me.* Then deep within his soul he felt guilty for the thought, but guilt has no place in the animal kingdom.

Remembering back to a peaceful time of innocence before the war during high school, he recalled a quote from J.D. Salinger's *Catcher in the Rye*: *'A wild animal lives its whole life, and never once feels sorry for itself. Even as it draws its last breath.'*

"To hell with guilt!" he screamed. "At least I'm still here and I'm not going home, whether it's in a plastic bag, walking, or crawling, until as many of you fuckers pay for this as possible!!"

Chapter 4

EDDY, BACK TO HIS PRESENT assignment, saw the village, quiet and slumbering. There were about ten thatched-roof hoochs spread over a relatively small area, with one larger in the middle. The sleepy nature was only natural, as it was about zero six hundred hours, and Charlie was only known to rise this early if he was going to attack, which was never done from a base this far into Cambodia let alone a command base.

As the sun hadn't crested the top of the surrounding mountains, the strong morning shadows still hung like a curtain dropped to conceal a secret of nature. Eddy had to use a starlight scope to distinguish detail. This particular piece of modern technology was new and rather barbaric. It was a single tube telescope that captured the infrared light waves so one could actually see in the dark. It cast a black and green image, so the scope took a little getting used to.

Basically, it reflected the heat signature from living matter. Not a bad piece of equipment advantage, especially since Charlie didn't have any.

Eddy saw a figure come out of one of the hoochs and walk toward the jungle. It stopped and put its hands in front of itself about hip high. The starlight scope showed a thin line of heat extending from his hip region, which arched downward toward the ground. Eddy laughed to himself as he realized that this particular light display was nothing more than some dumb moron taking a piss.

As this event proceeded, the sun was slowly starting to cause the starlight scope to become ineffectual. So, Eddy put it away and used, in its place, the high-powered scope on his AK 50.

To his surprise, the individual with the temporary bladder problem was the Colonel. He turned, as he was finishing his morning shakedown, and spoke back at the hooch. Eddy moved the scope to observe whom he was talking to.

There, in the opening that served as a door, was a young girl. Probably a girl taken from a local village and turned into the Colonel's whore, to be used and shared among the North Vietnamese as he saw fit. She couldn't have been more than twelve or thirteen years old and barely a woman. This, of course, wouldn't have stopped the Colonel. His reputation was that he did what he wanted to whomever he wanted, and didn't care.

Most animals have a survival instinct. Humans are no different. Eddy thought that any women who believed they were above such things, that they would never succumb to such activity to simply stay alive or keep some member of their family from being tortured or killed, is living under the same illusion that lets them believe that the human animal cares for anything other than itself.

"Take care of the one person guaranteed to be at your funeral!!" This was a saying passed down from old-timers to FNGs and ingrained in a combat vet's thinking process.

Eddy knew from the depths of his soul that man is capable of anything. And the simple act of a woman spreading her legs and letting a man stick his dick into her, or having to gratify a man with oral sex would keep her alive, was well within reason.

Believe it! No woman would hesitate long enough to notice. Only in the over protected life lived in America do women, out of pure ignorance and self-delusion, or an illusion of self-worth, stand and vomit their stupidity by making such statements like, "Oh, I'd never do something like that!" Or, "That girl must be a real slut. I'd rather die first!"

Let them look down the business end of an AK 47. Or let them watch a loved one being skinned alive.

Literally skinned alive.

Being skinned alive is where an incision is made in the skin with a knife and then the fingers are inserted into the cut grabbing the skin, followed by its being torn away with strong pulling jerks, ripped from its surrounding tissue. All while the person is conscious, and all without painkiller in any form, screaming from the Bowels of Hell.

Eddy knew, because he had seen it all, anyone would do anything. The veneer of civilization is very thin, and it doesn't take much to make it vanish. How far we have evolved from the beast is measured in such small fractions it would take an electron microscope to measure it.

The Colonel yelled at the girl. She jumped and started to go back into the hooch. He yelled again and she stopped, turned around and walked over to him. She seemed to have nothing on but a blanket she had wrapped around herself. As she approached the Colonel, he backhanded her across the mouth. She fell back onto the ground releasing her grip on the blanket. As it fell from her small body, Eddy could see that he had hit her before, many times. The bruises were large and plentiful.

As the Colonel stood over her she twisted her naked body to try and fend off any further blows. The Colonel bent down and slapped her a couple of times, then started to kick her. Over and over again the kicks continued until Eddy was about ready to blow this asshole away right then and there. After all, he had him in his sight. All he had to do was squeeze off one round. Orders or no orders, he couldn't take seeing anyone abused this way.

Screw the mission, he thought. *Just one round!*

Unfortunately, the Russian Major ran out of the hooch and pushed the Colonel away from the girl just as Eddy was sighting his rifle. He dropped the rifle and picked up his binos to see better. He wanted to know what the hell was going on.

The Major stood there, between the girl and the Colonel, yelling. The Colonel yelled back. This seemed to arouse the entire camp as soldiers started coming out of other hoochs in various stages of dress to gather around the three.

Noticing the circle of men around them, the Major stopped yelling, reached down, grabbed the girl by the arm, and pulled her to her feet. He then picked up the blanket, wrapped it around her, and led her back into the hooch. The men slowly went back to what they were doing as the Colonel stood there shouting. Evidently, he had turned his frustration from the Major to his men.

Eddy thought, *What an asshole!* Yes, he was looking forward to taking this guy out.

Eddy pulled his group back to go over any last minute changes to the plan he thought might be necessary to allow for new developments. There were no changes so they set the time to start the operation. Everyone was to be in position in exactly ten minutes. This would give them the ability to take advantage of the soldier's distraction caused by the argument, which had just ensued.

There is an ancient Vietnamese proverb, *"In order to kill the tiger, you have to lure him from his lair."* Eddy was going to have to get the Colonel out of that encampment if his mission was to be successful.

G-2 Intelligence had done their job and documented the method of operation the Colonel used during his normal activities. Where they got this information, Eddy didn't know nor did he care. They had their ways and he had his.

The plan was to have the Montagnards go out to the opening of the valley and create a diversion of some kind. This would cause the North Vietnamese soldiers to investigate. The Colonel would follow as far as the edge of the village where he would wait for the patrol to report back as to the cause of the disturbance. Eddy would be positioned at an exact location for optimum advantage. He'd chosen a spot behind a fallen tree that would not only give him cover, but offered a perfect support to rest his weapon. When the target is a long distance away, it is mandatory to have a support of some kind. The slightest movement would cause a miss. At a thousand yards, a shift at the muzzle of less than an eighth of an inch would cause a miss measured in feet.

There, he would take out the Colonel, and Mal and Steve would be in position near the Major's hooch to rush in and snatch him. Mal had the drugs and syringe to render him unconscious so he couldn't sound an alarm or give any unnecessary trouble.

Mal and Steve had been in country for a few months before Eddy arrived and knew what they were doing. He fully trusted and relied on the two to cover his *six*. A team acts and thinks as one. The three achieved this goal very quickly. War does that to a person. There is no time for a learning curve. You either learn quickly, or you die.

They learned quickly.

The plan was simple enough. It had worked before. So why did Eddy feel strange this particular time? What had been over looked? What was different?

God, he thought. *A guy could go crazy from the paranoia alone.*

He sent the Montagnards on their way and Mal and Steve on theirs. After a ten-count he slowly crawled back to his observation post to watch the camp. He didn't want to move into his kill-spot too early. It never was a good idea to be very long in one location let alone the specific place where a small piece of hollowed lead was to very soon become a deadly projectile. It had one purpose: to grab as much brain tissue as possible on its one-way trip from the brass cartridge held within the AK-50 to ultimately end in the jungle behind.

His was a rifle specially machined to take up all the slop creating a far more accurate piece of equipment while still giving off the familiar sound of a weapon used by the North Vietnamese. It had the additional advantage of giving Eddy the ability to replace his ammo supply from the munitions taken off of dead enemy.

When the time was right Eddy crawled to his pre-determined location where he would sight in on the exact spot where the Colonel would take his last breath in this world.

Suddenly, from the open end of the valley there came the sounds of rifle fire and people yelling. Eddy looked at his watch. Something was wrong. It was too early. The diversion wasn't supposed to take place for another three or four minutes. The Montagnards were known for following orders and being on time.

What the hell could have happened? Eddy very quickly got his answer. And, he knew what he had missed. He'd forgotten to do a head count of the soldiers in the camp.

A squad of North Vietnamese Regulars chose just that particular time to come back from a mission. As the Montagnards were setting up their little diversion, the North Vietnamese came upon them. If you had ever seen a Montagnard you know there was no confusing the two races. The Vietnamese and the Montagnards have never liked one another.

Any race in America who thinks that they are being picked on or discriminated against should see the abject and blatant bigotry the Vietnamese show toward the Montagnard. A Vietnamese can, in cold blood, kill a Montagnard in the middle of the street and no one will even stop to notice. The body would eventually be dragged away and thrown on a garbage heap.

And, that is, only if the Montagnard was lucky.

It was instantly obvious to the North Vietnamese that these Montagnards didn't belong here, and that they were up to no good. They executed one of them, and hamstrung the other. (That's another little love-kiss the Vietnamese liked to do to captives. They cut the Achilles tendon so the prisoner can't run.) Then they dragged him into the camp.

Well, you can imagine that by this time, between the shouting and the shooting, the camp was at full alert. Sleeping soldiers in various states of dress were pouring out of their hoochs, pulling up pants, and tugging on shirts. The poor Montagnard who was dragged in definitely had the Colonel's attention, and the Major's.

Eddy couldn't get a clean shot from his present location. He had to move, so he crawled to a place beside a large rock where he could take out the Colonel.

As he was steadying his rifle he noticed the Colonel kicking and beating the Montagnard. Eddy knew he was trying to get him to talk, to tell what he was doing there and if there were any others. The tough little guy wouldn't say a word. To Eddy's horror, the Colonel pulled a knife and cut the Montagnard across the chest, then grabbed the skin of the open wound and pulled.

No one knows the sound a human can make when they experience the torments of Hell on Earth!

As trained as Eddy was, as experienced, as dedicated to the mission and focused, something inside of him snapped. This little brown soldier in the loincloth had been a good man. He had laughed and joked with Eddy. He had shared his home and his wife had cooked for him. He's the one that taught Eddy how to make a crossbow. It was this brave man that stood with him on the top of the hill challenging the NVA after the foiled attack on the Korean Battery during TET. He had five children and worked his rice paddy to provide for his family. He was a loving and caring husband and father. Bai Son didn't deserve *this*.

Instantly Eddy moved the sight slightly, his eyes fixed on his target, and he fired. Bai Son slumped over -- dying instantly. Eddy couldn't stand to see his little friend tortured. If he was to die, Eddy made sure it was quick and by his hands, not that bastard's. He had stopped the pain. The bullet intended for the Colonel passed through the Montagnard. Eddy's internal pain was so great he didn't even remember pulling the trigger, but training and instinct usually take over. It was common to undergo self-hypnosis when one is a sniper. It's the only way to maintain a fingernail hold on sanity. And how much of a hold has been debated by many. Psychological tombs have been written on what makes up someone capable of doing the job.

An experienced soldier, the Colonel instantly hit the ground and rolled to cover. Eddy's second round missed. The rule is: One shot, one kill. You never took a second. And here, Eddy had broken numerous rules. An unforgiveable mistake. North Vietnamese soldiers flooded out of the camp and fanned out surrounding the village.

"OK, hero!" Eddy mumbled to himself sarcastically knowing that the last thing on earth he wanted to be was a hero. Most heroes were recognized for their heroism posthumously, a condition that Eddy wasn't quite ready for. "How are you going to get out of this mess? And where are Mal and Steve?"

He immediately started looking for a spot to hide. There! A tree had fallen years ago and under the trunk was a small indentation in the ground creating a shallow cave of a sort. It was just big enough to hold his body if he balled up tight.

He crawled in and covered his exposed parts with leaves and foliage from the jungle floor. Unless the gooks scraped off the ground debris they would never see him. The pile looked natural.

Concentrating, he slowed his breathing down and lay as still as death. This was a talent required for anyone doing the job. Regardless of the surrounding circumstances, you controlled your breathing, slowing it down calming the entire body. The slightest noise could be heard in the jungle by those used to hearing normal sounds.

He lay there. Quiet. Rain began to patter on the leaves and smack against the ground. So much for the weather report and Eddy was glad for it.

It's not even called rain. It has a special name: *Monsoons.*

Eddy knew the name came from the British that occupied India for so many years. It referred to the big winds blowing in from the Bay of Bengal. But now it was a term for the seasonal reversing wind and corresponding change in precipitation. He knew this but, as a matter of fact, didn't care. We was happy for the added visual and auditory screening. He did, however, recall the first time he'd experienced the torrential phenomenon.

Remembering back to when he had only been *in country* (the expression all GIs used meaning *in Viet Nam*) a little while, maybe a couple of weeks, when he partook of the wet welcome that Godforsaken, useless piece of real estate gave to all those who didn't have any better sense than to think that there was anything in this part of the world worth fighting and dying for.

But, there he was, *fighting for his country.*

Eddy did what he thought was right. Growing up watching all the World War II movies where *Johnny comes marching home from serving his country's call.* Proudly wearing his uniform. Instantly getting the respect of all his countrymen. Welcomed with open arms to any job of his choice. Always getting the girl because they loved a man in uniform.

Something every Viet Nam Vet learned very quickly was a lot of bullshit.

His first experience with a monsoon was actually quite funny. There he was, busy digging a large hole in the ground with five other luckless chaps. The hole had to be about eight to ten feet on a side and about four feet deep. Then with a five-stack of sandbags and a roof made of bamboo and more sandbags, he and the other fools would have a bunker to sleep in and run like hell to, whenever Charlie decided to be cute and attack with rockets, mortars, AK 47s, grenades, and anything else he could throw at them.

All of a sudden it started to rain. At first Eddy welcomed it, as the humidity was unbearable. You couldn't breathe it was so bad. Different from the clean smell, which permeates the air just after a rain in the U.S., it was the sick, putrid smell of decomposition. Everything got wet and stayed wet, rotting in the process. Everything -- including your skin. A soldier had to be careful. If you allowed your skin to stay wet *jungle rot* would set in.

Jungle rot is where the skin can't dry and starts to rot. You had to change your socks every night. You never wore underwear. The reason for this little bit of trivia is because your clothes got soaked every day. The only way to dry them was to sleep in them allowing one's body heat to cause water in the saturated cloth to evaporate while you slept. If you wore underwear, the body heat never got to the cloth. You stayed wet.

Regarding the humidity. If you add heavy labor to the seeming lack of oxygen, you start to understand the Vietnamese. You'd be all messed-up in the head too if this was the best your life could offer.

All of the guys that had been in country awhile dropped what they were doing, stripped completely, grabbed their soap, and started to wash. A nice fragrant deodorant soap was never used. The last thing anyone wanted was to alert Charlie of their presence in the jungle by the out-of-place smell of *lilac bouquet*.

Eddy, not knowing what was going on, stood there for a moment wondering what the hell everyone was doing. All the GIs, except the FNGs, which he was, were naked as the day they were born, standing on top of their bunkers, washing in the rain.

Eddy stopped for a moment in his memory while hiding under the log and wondered how different, or perhaps more pleasant, it would have been if women were allowed in the fighting units back then. Showers would have probably been a lot slower.

Anyway, when he asked what they were doing, he received the reply that that was the only chance he had to get clean. So, not wanting to stink any worse than everyone else, Eddy grabbed his soap, stripped, and started to scrub.

Now, you see, one little problem with being a FNG:
NO ONE EXPLAINS ANYTHING *BEFORE* IT HAPPENS!!!!!

Just as fast as the rains start, they stop. This happened just as Eddy got all lathered-up.

No rain!

No rinse!!

No shit!!!

He stayed with crusted soap on his body for two days until that damn country decided it had made every living organism sufficiently miserable with the humidity to allow the rain to begin again.

Eddy didn't hesitate the next time. He wouldn't have cared if General Westmoreland's virgin daughter were standing there talking to him. When the rain started, he was naked and rinsing.

The rain was warm and came down hard. Sometimes so hard you couldn't see five feet in front of you. Not that there was anything you wanted to see. You couldn't hear either. Yelling at the guy less than a foot from you was commonplace. Charlie loved it. He could sneak in, snipe, and leave. You couldn't see him and you couldn't hear him. All you could do was bag your dead friend, who one moment was sitting next to you talking about life and the next he's on the ground with a bullet hole in him, then send him home. Nothing about this country was good.

Nothing!

It was weird what a guy thinks about when he's scared and wondering if he's going to die. Once again, Eddy was happy it was coming down.

Time seemed to pass very slowly. Seconds became minutes. Minutes became hours. How long did he lie under the log? He really didn't know. He didn't bother to look at his watch. Time was on his side. He knew that much. The longer he evaded detection the better off he was. They would eventually give up, figuring he had escaped and was long gone. Then he could quietly slip away to a safe distance where he could determine the disposition of the rest of his team.

What a dumb-ass he had been. *How professional are you?* he asked himself as he lay motionless under the log thinking over what had happened--trying to make sense of how everything went wrong. *You know better than to do what you did. A private in basic training knows better. Your buddy wasn't going anywhere. He was being skinned alive for Christ's sake! You should have taken out the Colonel first, and then changed positions before firing the shot to end the little guy's suffering. One round, no one knows where it comes from. The second, everyone knows the location. So what did you do? Like a total amateur, you got caught up in the dangerous emotion of caring for a friend in wartime and allowed it to mess you up.*

Gee! he continued to ask himself sarcastically, *I wonder how they were able to get an idea approximately where you were. If I get out of this mess,* he continued as in prayer, *I will never care for another person. Caring only screws up your judgment.*

I just wonder if I will get out of this.

His answer came quicker than he would have liked. As he lay there, suddenly something clamped on to his leg. He was quickly dragged out from under the log. As his eyes adjusted to the light, after being in the dark for so long, he saw that he was surrounded by a Vietnamese patrol. The Russian Major was standing directly over him holding a rifle, butt down.

The last thing he remembered was everything happening in slow motion. He watched the Major raise the rifle up, and then with great force brought it down on his head. The lights went out and Eddy slept. In a way it was a relief. The hell he had been witness to, the horror he had seen, the pain he had observed inflicted on humans, the pain he himself had inflicted on other humans -- all gone. Everything was peaceful.

And Eddy slept.

Chapter 5

EDDY WOULD HAVE, AT THAT moment of his existence, been quite content to die, to continue the sleep for all eternity. But such was not his destiny, or so it seemed. He was brought out of his peaceful slumber quite rudely by having water thrown on him, followed immediately by some very hard slaps across the face.

As his mind started to register the real world that once again was being thrust upon him, he detected someone yelling. He couldn't see. His eyes wouldn't open. But the screams slowly became audible and seemed to be emanating from the same person inflicting the slaps. He tried to raise his hand to ward off the abuse. It was beginning to get rather painful the more he woke up. But, he couldn't. Maybe he was paralyzed and his arms wouldn't work.

Yes, that must be it.

Now he remembered. Somehow he must have gotten away and back to a friendly outfit. Maybe he had been wounded in the skirmish and ended up paralyzed in the process. He must have been transported to a hospital and the medical personnel were trying to get him to come out of the anesthesia from the surgery they had performed.

Yeah! That's it! he thought excitedly. *I'm not really paralyzed. Just restrained during surgery so I won't hurt myself. Probably got tripped by the dog... or ran over a hose. Maybe, my wisdom teeth grew back and needed to come out again...*

Why didn't the house paint last longer than five years?

Oh, yeah. Fords do have four tires. They should. They have four wheels, for God's sake. I mean, if they didn't have the same amount of tires as they do wheels...? That's absolutely right! No garlic!

No garlic, and no French bread for French toast... Or is it French fries? I don't know. But, I sure would like to have gotten my hands on Melinda. God, she was beautiful.

And popular, too.

Wham! Another blow to the face followed immediately by water being thrown again, then another hit.

Honest, Melinda, I only brought you to the beach so we could enjoy the day. I wasn't getting fresh. If I wanted to grab your tits, I wouldn't have just casually rubbed my hand against one of them as we lay on the beach towels. I would have taken both of those gorgeous weapons of womanhood and swallowed them all the way to the spine. You didn't have to hit me. It was an accident.

Wham! Whack! Two more.

Wait a minute, he continued. *Those hits are pretty hard for a woman to have dealt the blows. Of course, I've seen some pretty healthy women. In fact, I dated a girl once. What was her name? Coreen? Claudette? Carmen? Miranda? She could really dance with those bananas on her head.*

Not bananas -- bandanas. The kind my brother and I wore when we would run up to our neighbor's back doors at night. Then, putting a small piece of tape with a picture of a bat on it on the doorframe, ring the bell or pound on the wood, and run like hell. Yes, they would know and hide in fear from the Order of the Bat *Club.*

Wham!!!

That was more like the baseball type of bat inflicting the pain than by a little furry flying creature.

More water! ...and again!

Finally Eddy's senses started to grasp reality. *And none too soon,* he thought groggily.

"OK! OK! I'm awake. What do you want?" he asked realizing that he was tied tightly to a pole. His hands had gone to sleep from lack of circulation. His legs seemed unable to hold up his weight, which was actually no big thing as his legs weren't the supporting part of his body anyway. A bamboo rod went under both of his armpits and behind the pole creating a type of cross. He almost felt as though he was being crucified without the use of nails.

Lucky him!

Instead of nails, bamboo stakes about a quarter of an inch wide by four inches long and sharpened to a fine point, were used. They had a tendency to splinter. But, what the hell. He was only an American -- and every Gook knew *Americans had no real feelings.*

The bamboo spikes were driven through the pole just under the armpits extending about three quarters of an inch from the pole. Any movement would cause the point to pierce the tender skin, and then possibly break off. This eventually would cause a tremendous infection, as the spikes had been urinated on or rubbed in shit before being pounded into the pole.

But, of course, this didn't matter at all. Eddy figured he would be dead long before the bacteria would even begin spreading through his body.

The hard part of torture was keeping the victim awake and alive. During his Black Ops training at Langley, he had been fully versed on torture techniques. He was always happy that he had never been called upon to perform any of them. That knowledge wasn't doing him a lot of good at this moment as he was the one being tortured and was aware just how long he could endure. He would have to call on every devise he'd been taught to simply make it to the next moment. Tomorrow would take care of itself.

Pain did no good to someone who was out cold and couldn't feel anything, or to someone who had the unmitigated, discourteous, and uncooperative gall to die. Some victims just didn't understand the concept. A person being tortured had to know he was being subjected to incredible pain. The victim had to scream, yell, cry, and plead. Otherwise, it just wasn't any fun.

Last thing I want to do is spoil someone's idea of an E-Ticket ride, Eddy thought as he came fully awake.

"OK, OK, dick-heads. I'm awake. So stop the monsoon and the bitch-slapping."

As he tried to open his eyes he realized they were caked shut with blood, probably from the head injury caused by the rifle butt. As more water was thrown on his face it eventually washed away the blood and he was able to see a little. He had been brought into the camp and was held in the larger central hooch which was about fifteen feet wide by thirty feet long and about seven feet high at the walls, then slanted upward to a peak about ten feet off the floor. It was made of log braces and supports with the thatch roof. Actually, it was bamboo leaves piled on top of one another,

There were three men in the room with him, the Colonel, who was doing the yelling, and two line soldiers, who were the ones taking turns hitting and throwing water. All were smiling and laughing.

Of course, Eddy wasn't smiling at all. But then again, he was the one whose body was being destroyed. So, the act of pulling back the corners of one's mouth and displaying the teeth in a sign of joy or humor wasn't the first reaction on his mind. Getting free and practicing at least a dozen of the one hundred and twenty-five some-odd ways of brutally killing these little assholes was a much more pleasant thought.

Suddenly a new voice rang out in the din. "Enough!" The voice had such authority the gooks froze mid-swing. All eyes, including Eddy's, turned toward the source of the command.

Standing just inside the door, then slowly walking over toward Eddy was the Russian Major. He noticed that the Major didn't seem happy about the goings on and had finally had his fill of these creatures with which he was ordered to work, but no power on the Earth could make him like, or respect.

One of the gooks yelled something back. The Major backhanded him across the mouth, knocking him on his ass. The other gook pulled his pistol and came at the Major.

He was stopped in his tracks instantly. Looking down, he noticed a knife protruding from his chest, which hadn't been there a moment before. He dropped his pistol and grabbed the knife hilt, trying to pull it out.

The Major knocked his hand away and at the same time, pushed the hilt causing the blade to cut sideways and directly into the heart.

The gook looked up slowly at the Major with his mouth gaping open, eyes rolling up and back as he sank to the floor. The Major grabbed the knife and twisting clockwise, extracted it from its bloody sheath.

As the Russian was wiping it off on the dead man's body, the Colonel took a step toward him, and then stopped. The Russian had pulled his pistol and the muzzle was pressed against the Colonel's forehead.

"Don't even think of it," he calmly said almost in a whisper. Strangely enough, they were speaking English although the Major had a very heavy Russian dialect. "They were wrong and so are you. He is a human being. Not an animal you can just beat and treat any way you want. He has an honor I'm sure you know nothing about. What he did, though very foolish, showed it.

"I will kill anyone who harms him. He deserves better. Also, he undoubtedly knows a lot of information. He's much more valuable alive than dead...or senseless. I'll take him north for interrogation."

"Not alone, you won't," responded the Colonel in perfect English trying to assert his authority. "I don't trust you any more than I trust him. I will go with you to ensure he arrives and is properly questioned. Remember, Major, you are a guest in my country. We do not like taking orders from you any more than we like being the servants of the Americans or, before them, the French.

"We are the race that is destined to control the world, not you. We are strong and our numbers are many. Your pathetic people are weak. You worry about making life good. We, on the other hand, don't care about the quality of life. We will receive our comforts after death. So, we quietly populate the world. If we are to be defeated in this little war, so be it. There will be other wars.

"Your pitiful Western religions have been thrust on us by missionaries for hundreds of years. All they have succeeded in doing is giving us the determination to continue the struggle. This *Christ* that is talked about so much, who is believed to be the Son of God, is a perfect example of your weakness.

"You see Major, I have studied this nonsense. Christ turned the other cheek when he got slapped. Keep doing that and you run out of cheeks.

"It was because of your white missionaries, spouting a feeble religion that speaks of brotherly love, that loved my people so much they sold us out to the French who used us no better than slaves.

"No, Major. Your race will not inherit this Earth. Mine will. It is better that you remember that. Be on the winning side. Then at least your heirs will be more favored. Who knows? Maybe your grandchildren could have a favored position in my grandchildren's house or business.

"Just remember. We will be the over-seers. You will be the laborers."

Then with a raising of his head, and literally sticking his nose in the air, he took a large inhale, nodded, then continued. "It is better that way."

"Keep talking like that and you won't have to worry about looking forward to the life you live after death. I'll introduce you to it right now. And what about these two?" He pointed to the two soldiers on the floor.

"What about them?" responded the Colonel. "They have done their duty to the Party. We'll get replacements when we get to Hanoi."

"You're a real piece of shit, Nguyen," stated the Major. "How the hell did you get a position of authority in the Army? Did they run out of sane people? Get out."

With that, the Major lowered his pistol and put it back into its holster. The Colonel shrugged, and turned to leave. Walking out he said, "I'm not the one doing a job I obviously don't want to do. Who's the insane one?" Then he left.

The Major pivoted and strode over to Eddy. Picking up a rag, he wiped some of the water and blood off of Eddy's face. Then he cut his bindings and lifted him off the *cross*.

"I hope you don't give me any trouble. I hate the little bastards, but I will do my job if I have to. Cooperate, and you won't be hurt anymore. They don't own the world, yet. But, if you fail to cooperate, it will be out of my hands. As you can see, the alternative is less than pleasant. I'm just glad it was me that found you. They would have probably killed you. All I did was knock you out. I hope I didn't hurt you too badly. I tried to pull the punch.

"By the way, were you going to kill me, too? If you were, saving you would have been rather stupid, and I am not a stupid persons.

"No," replied Eddy cautiously. "We were to capture you and take you back as proof of Soviet presence in Southeast Asia."

"Interesting. I would like to have seen that attempt. That would have proven a lot. It has to happen this way. If you had asked, I would probably have gone with you and everything would be different. These are terrible people. Only bad things can happen with them. I don't understand why Mother Russia cannot see this." He shook his head in disgust.

"What do you mean?" asked Eddy. "What has to happen what way?"

"Never mind. By the way, the next time you dig in to hide under a tree trunk, try not to leave a piece of your clothing on the trunk directly over you." He pulled a piece of camouflage cloth out of his pocket and tossed it to Eddy.

"I'll keep it in mind," Eddy responded, totally confused. "As for my cooperating, I highly doubt that any part of what lies in store for me will be pleasant, but thank you anyway." Eddy was having a hard time believing the sincerity of the Major, while desperately wanting to. It could be a *Good guy - Bad guy* routine, but at least the beating had stopped and there were two gooks lying on the floor, one with his life-force oozing through the floorboards of the hooch, the other still out cold or dead -- probably the latter. This bear of a man must pack one hell of a punch. Christ knows he's big enough.

Chapter 6

THE DAYS PASSED, AS DID the weeks. Eddy was kept in a cage made of bamboo and submerged most of the way into the river that ran along the village.

Now, this was not a beautiful sparkling river, which ambles over stone and stick containing trout and crayfish, pure, clean, and refreshing. It did not call to the inner senses and say, *Pull out the fly-rod and cast into me so I can sing my peace onto your heart.*

No. It was a putrid source of brown and green filth moving from one location to another containing all forms of waste and garbage. In this luxury suite, he never got any real sleep. If he nodded off, his head would sink under the water. Unable to breath, he would snap awake coughing and gagging. The human body had a very strong urge to continue to breathe. The urge to sleep was secondary, but necessary.

Eddy finally found a way to catch a few winks by wedging his head between two of the bamboo bars, which had become slightly loose. Once wedged, he could let himself disappear into oblivion for a moment or two.

He didn't worry about being killed while he slept. He figured he probably wasn't going to get out alive anyway, so what the hell. Most Viet

Nam vets gave up the idea of coming home alive shortly after arriving in country, so this wasn't a recent conclusion.

More than a few times he was rudely woken up by one of the gooks doing something to him, and that something was never pleasant. One unforgettable moment was when he was snapped out of his sleep by a feeling of something mushy hitting his up-turned face. As he opened his eyes, it took a moment to register what he was looking at. There, not a foot from his eyes and just above the bamboo bars was an asshole. Out of this sphincter shit was flowing.

He didn't know why this came as such a surprise. His luxury apartment must have been accidentally placed over the latrine. Why else would all the gooks, whenever they had to relieve themselves, run over to where he was and piss or shit on him? You would think this in itself would be disgusting enough. But remember, the NVA didn't enjoy three balanced meals a day. Their human waste made normal defecation smell good in comparison.

Eddy's skin was starting to show the effect of being submerged in water for too long a period. His only break came when he was hauled out for his periodic questioning, subsequent torture, and beatings.

Every hour, at least three times in the hour, he was told to prepare himself for his execution. Then it never came. Eddy was getting to the point where he wished it would. They can only kill him once. Torture never stops.

The tortures usually happened when the Major was not around for some reason. His torment came with many faces: beatings with slivered bamboo, slow cuts opening his flesh followed by urine or salt in the wound, being hooked up to an electric generator and having the volts increased slowly, being bent over backwards and having water constantly poured on his upturned face and into his nose until he thought he were drowning, being bent into positions the human body was never meant to be placed in and held for hours at a time, having his feet beaten until they were a bloody mess and he couldn't walk, having bamboo splinters slowly inserted under the fingernails, God only knew what inserted into his rectum so far Eddy thought it would come out his mouth.

Nice afternoons like that.

Then, when the Colonel had enough enjoyment for the day, he was returned to his watery resort. Sometimes this entailed being dragged and dropped in the cage. Beneath his torn fatigues his flesh was wrinkling and softening as it was subjected to the constant moisture. His open wounds soaked up the bacteria from the stinking river. A periodic leach would attach itself on to drain some of the life force the Vietnamese left behind. As disgusting as these scavengers were, the Vietnamese were worse. At least the leaches were part of nature. They had some purpose to exist on the planet. Eddy couldn't think of a single beneficial purpose to life that these Vietnamese served.

His one hold on mental peace was the belief that Mal and Steve had gotten away safely. Or rather, he hoped they had. No mention was made about any of his party being killed. The NVA never hesitated in bragging about killing a GI.

Two months after he had been captured, by his best account of time, he was dragged out of his cage. A bamboo rod was shoved under his arms running behind him. Then his hands were tied in front of his stomach with the rope running between his legs and up to his neck. There, it was looped around and tied before going down to one ankle and the other with just enough slack so he could walk. He was loaded with supplies like a pack animal and made to stand on a trail leading out of the base camp.

A collar made of bamboo that had been soaked in water and bent into a circle then dried was placed around his neck. The bamboo was not smoothed. The edges with the dry, brittle fibers were as sharp as needles and constantly stabbed and cut his neck.

As he stood there, he became aware that bamboo rods attached his collar to others behind him. More people were being added to this out-of-style accessory. He couldn't see as he was the point man and the way he was tied kept him from turning around.

So, he thought, *they have more prisoners. It must be a real sight, all of us here, looking like Charlton Heston going to the Roman Galleys in Ben Hur. Only this is no movie... and these are no Romans. They don't even qualify as humans.*

Eddy asked himself, *Has man ever been kind to his fellow man?*

The Colonel walked up to the front of the column and looked it over. Then he approached Eddy, smiled, and asked, "Are you wondering where we are going? Would you like to know?"

"If you want me to know something, I have no doubt you will tell me. My wanting to know doesn't matter. Now, does it?"

"You're as insolent as you are stupid," responded the Colonel. "But, since I seem to get an enormous pleasure out of seeing you in pain, I will tell you. Then, I have a little surprise for you. I've been saving it for months. The stupid Major thought you might not like surprises, but I just couldn't resist."

"Goody," Eddy responded with full sarcastic force.

"You," the Colonel continued ignoring the sarcasm, "are being taken into North Viet Nam. You needn't worry about being rescued or us being attacked, as we will at no time be in the South. We will continue in Cambodia until we get next to the North, then we will cross over. Eventually you will take up residence in the prisoner of war camp in Hanoi. That is, if you are still alive. I believe you Americans refer to it as the Hanoi Hilton, quite a pet name and actually very complimentary. You see, I have spent a lot of time in your country and have stayed in many of the Hilton hotels. Very nice.

"I actually received an education there, you know. I was given it free of charge by your government as a part of the student exchange program.

"I did my undergraduate work at Berkley then went on to get a Master's at Stanford. All paid by your idiotic government. Or should I say, by the American taxpayer.

"Want to know what I majored in?" continued the Colonel.

Eddy really hated this waste of humanity. He didn't have to learn to hate him. It was coming quite naturally.

"Ummmm," answered Eddy. "Let me guess." He imagined if he said something offensive like he wanted to the Colonel would probably fly off the handle again and do something painful, as he had done so many times before. It was almost a routine. Be a smart-ass with the Colonel, and you get beaten. Really be offensive, and the pain corresponds.

"*Hell the what*", he said. He liked to turn phrases around. It helped keep him sane. "What're you going to do, send me to Viet Nam?

"I know!" he continued. "You studied anatomy so you could tell the difference between your head and your asshole."

Whack!! The Colonel cracked his command stick across Eddy's face.

"Wrong guess, huh?" continued Eddy spitting blood from his mouth. He knew again that you could only die once. "OK. I'm sorry. That was stupid of me to have thought of the sciences. You're more of an imaginary thinker than a man of logic. You would have indulged in a field where your mind could really take off. How about waste management? I mean -- you *are* full of shit."

Bam! Whack! Slam!

"Wrong again, I guess. I'm not very good at this. Am I?" he continued not knowing when to quit. He was noticing some laughter coming from the Vietnamese who had overheard his remarks and understood English. This just made him want to continue more.

Anything for a laugh! Nothing, however, came from the others tied behind him.

"All right. All right! I get one more try. Oh, for Christ's sake! Of course! God, am I stupid! I mean, a fool would have known. You started by majoring in masturbation, but had to change majors due to the fact that you couldn't find your little cock, you dickless du miami...!"

Wham!!! Kick!!!!

"Then finally got your degree in Geology, by letting all the fags, dồng tình luyên ái, excavate your anal cave, you buggered son of a bitch!"

Bam!! Bam!! Bam!! Whack!! Pow!!

"Then got your Master's in stupidity, do to your head being so far up your ass, you puny little twerp.

"So, fuck you and your education! Fuck you and your major! Fuck you and your surprise! Come to think of it, just FUCK YOU!!!"

The Colonel started beating and kicking him so badly he finally collapsed to the ground pulling his fellow prisoners with him. The kicking continued with more force and the furious screams from the Colonel were so fierce that Eddy thought this time he just might have gone too far. It just might be a good day to die.

It was at this moment that the Colonel started stomping on his hand with the heel of his boot. He kept it up until the flesh was torn away exposing the bone. Then he took out his pistol and held it point blank at Eddy's head. He stood over him. To Eddy, it seemed forever. Then just when he thought he was going to die, he heard the Major's voice screaming at the Colonel, threatening him to leave Eddy alone or he would personally, right then and there, rid the world of his insanity.

The Colonel, looking up seeing the Major running toward him, removed the gun from Eddy's head, put it against the back of his mangled hand as it lay in the dirt.

"So that you will always remember me, Pig!" screamed the madman, he squeezed the trigger.

That was the last time Eddy had full use of that hand.

Chapter 7

IT DIDN'T HURT AS MUCH as Eddy thought it should, probably because the Colonel's boot had destroyed all the nerves in his hand. But it sure looked like hell and it was going to be really hard to pick his nose from then on.

He held it up and looked at it.

Thinking back, Eddy imagined what a sight he must have been laying there in the dirt. Beaten into a mess, he slowly sat up, blood dripping from his face, eyes swollen almost shut. He raised his hand and looked through the hole the bullet had made. Like looking through a knothole in a piece of wood, Eddy could see the Major standing over him.

"Nice shot," whispered Eddy, not quite able to find his voice. "Wouldn't you say so, Major? Kind of screwed-up my hand, but I have another one to jack-off with."

Then turning his head to look at the Colonel and finding his voice, said, "You had better finish me now, Nguyên. Giêt tôi!!! Kill me, because I *will* kill you. Tôi Giêt ông!!!!"

"Enough!" shouted the Major. "Anh ây sê bâng tay."

He pointed to one of the North Vietnamese soldiers who had gathered around, then to Eddy. He told the soldier to bandage Eddy's hand, but the

Vietnamese hesitated. The Major pulled his pistol and pointed it at him. Suddenly finding the incentive, he jumped to work on the hand. It wasn't a good or clean job, but it would stop the bleeding and do for the moment.

The Major turned to the Colonel and walked slowly up to him. He got to within a foot of the little bastard then stopped. Leaning down until his nose was almost touching the Colonel's, he said, "Nguyên, I'm going to say this only once, and I'm going to say it in angleeskee yaziyk, the English Language, so this soldier can understand. He won't have to kill you. I will!!! Last warning."

He then turned and walked away. The whole time the Colonel hadn't moved. He didn't seem scared. He actually seemed bored, as though he had grown tired of it all and wanted to get on with something else. Eddy thought this guy really believed he was superior to everyone. He swore an oath to himself that Colonel Nguyên would be *superiorly* dead if it was the last thing he did on this earth.

The North Vietnamese dragged him to his feet and back to his place in the column. It was then that he got a shock that almost sent him over the edge. There was Mal and Steve, tied, gagged, and blindfolded. They were the ones attached to his neck collar.

They had both been beaten severely with cuts, rips, and bruises, all in horrid profusion on their bodies. They weren't moving. Just standing there, heads hung down, as if they had literally been knocked senseless. Each had a blank look on their faces. Eddy knew if he could have seen their eyes, they would probably have stared right past him. They were both undoubtedly drugged.

He wondered why they didn't use drugs on him. Then he remembered it wasn't as much fun beating a man when he's drugged. When his mind is clear, the reaction to pain is much more acute. The screaming and the begging are like applause to an actor. That is, if the actor is a close relative of the Marquis de Sade.

Eventually the column started moving. This was the beginning of a very long walk. One of which, Eddy thought, he would never see the end. He was right, but not the way he imagined.

Every foot was like a mile -- every mile, a continent. The distance they were traveling from any sort of sanctuary intensified Eddy's pain from his hand and beating. He knew with every step his chances of returning to the life he had once cherished were getting slimmer and slimmer.

At the end of the first day the group set up camp. Eddy was given his normal food ration, a half of a bowl of rice. Sometimes, if he was lucky and the North Vietnamese were feeling generous, a little protein or perhaps potassium was added to the rice. This usually took the form of some jungle insect. Most were crushed, but some were still crawling. Eddy had to scramble to catch them before the best part of his meal got away. If the Vietnamese were not feeling quite so generous, he might be forced to eat rice that had been urinated or defecated in.

He never knew for sure which mixture caused the most violent projectile vomiting. He suspected the shit-a-roni rice. It really didn't matter because he threw up with them all. It was just that some was more violent than others.

At the end of the day, after his nightly regurgitation, he sat and watched for some sign of awareness in Mal or Steve. Resigning himself to the fact that the drugs they were given had done major damage to them both, he finally drifted off to sleep.

The gooks didn't let this go on for too long. Whoever was on guard kept himself awake by inflicting pain, which also kept Eddy awake.

Every morning was the same. The group would arise, come over to relieve their full bladders on the Americans, then be on their way proceeding north. As hard as it may be to believe, the smell eventually became normal.

Every night, the same ritual.

Mal and Steve had, over the days and much to Eddy's delight, slowly come out of their zombie-like trance. The Vietnamese probably ran out of drugs and figured the Americans had been beaten into submission and they didn't need any more.

Eddy, Mal, and Steve were not allowed to talk among themselves, but they communicated with slight gestures of the eyes and heads. It wasn't much, just enough for Eddy to learn that the other two were OK. No permanent damage. At least he didn't think there was.

One memorable night, Colonel Nguyên had the three lined up together. He chose this particular evening because the Major had gone out with the nightly patrol and wouldn't be there to protect them.

Eddy realized over the days that the Colonel was truly a coward. Not the type who is simply afraid to try something risky, but rather the type who only picks on the weak or helpless. In a one-on-one, he would crawl away like the rat he was. And that statement was insulting to the rat.

This particular night, after the Colonel had the three of them lined up, he made them pull down their pants. He then had his whore, who he brought along, stand in front of them and strip naked. To her great protest and his subsequent beating of her, he made her perform oral sex on each one of the GIs in turn. When she had gotten each one sufficiently aroused causing an erection, Colonel Nguyên would swat the swollen penis with a whip of shaved bamboo, cutting the flesh and causing bamboo splinters to be forced into the tender skin and tissue.

This horror was amplified by the laughter of the Vietnamese. Eddy suffered most as he was the last to receive the blessing. The others had passed out from the pain, so they were only subjected to their own hell not the hell of the others. That memory was to be Eddy's, and Eddy's alone.

As the girl was working on him, he tried with all of his might to think of something else. Anything!! He had to keep from getting an erection. If he could just stared at Colonel Nguyên's eyes with hatred and loathing that would do the trick.

He was wrong.

Eventually Eddy turned his eyes to the poor frightened girl. He really felt sorry for her. This wasn't her war. He was certain that she would prefer spending the rest of her simple life picking rice and having baby sans.

Once again, Eddy's feeling for his fellow man was his undoing. As he felt pity for the girl, his guard came down and his penis came up.

Now that is real pain! he thought as the Colonel whipped and cut. The last thing that entered his mind, before he too passed out was, *I'm going to kill this son-of-a-bitch, deader than dead!*

Brave thoughts for a prisoner of war being led through hell and to his welcomed death.

Chapter 8

TIME BECAME A BLUR. How long had Eddy been a prisoner? How long had they been walking north? He really didn't know. Between his passing out and being thrown into holes where he didn't know day from night, the passage of specific periods of time was nonexistent.

It could have been two weeks or two months. Neither Mal, Steve, nor Eddy knew. The frightening part was that they started not to care.

But, they *had* to care. The only hope they had, and Eddy knew it, was to escape. The three had no idea where they were, but they knew where they were going. The arrival at this particular destination must be prevented at all costs. Even if they lived, the chance of getting away lessened every day they got closer to the Hilton. Once they arrived, their chances would be zero.

The North Vietnamese went out on patrol more and more as time went on. As each night fell, and the number of them going out on ambush increased, the number staying behind decreased. At first, this puzzled Eddy.

One day after Colonel Nguyên had experimented with the pain threshold of a GI by having Eddy tied down and slowly passing a very sharp piece of bamboo through the skin of his arm tearing a cut about three to four inches long and a quarter of an inch wide, followed by the pouring of salt on the wound. Then laughing and declaring that it would ease the burning, he proceeded to urinate on it. The Colonel, feeling elated with sadistic joy, went out on night patrol.

Thinking as his men had, that he had beaten down the three into total submission, the Colonel was confident that it didn't take an entire company of North Vietnamese to guard three worthless American GIs, so he left three guards to watch Eddy, Mal, and Steve, while the rest went out.

Eddy knew that if the Vietnamese soldiers were going out, they had to be in South Viet Nam. No reason to do such a thing in Cambodia or North Viet Nam. Nguyên said they wouldn't be, but why should lying be exempt from his life of dishonor?

It was tonight or never; they had to get away. The odds were finally in their favor, three against three. Only Eddy's three had better training and definitely better motivation.

It was a clear night. The stars could be seen through the top of the jungle canopy. Eddy watched the stars and estimated the distance they would travel in an hour using this reference as his clock.

After the Colonel and his company had been gone for a couple of hours, and Eddy was sure they were out of distance to hear or respond, he set the escape in motion.

Doubling over on the ground he started to moan and cry in pain. His hands and feet were tied together so he didn't have much of a move to double up.

"Tôi ôm bênh! (I am sick!) Tôi cân bâc sî! (I need a doctor!) Tôi dang bi khó thó. (I'm having trouble breathing.) Bi dau! Bi dau! (It hurts! It hurts!)," Eddy cried.

The one guard on duty, while the others took turns sleeping, came rushing over to him. "Anh có sai gi? (You, what wrong?)

As he kicked at Eddy, the moans just continued to get worse. He leaned down and asked again, "Anh cô sai gi?"

Eddy groaned then weakly replied, "Tôi chúa có kinh tù ...tháng nay. (I haven't had my period for...months.)

The gook sat back startled, not believing he heard correctly. Eddy seized this moment to roll over onto him knocking him to the ground. As he continued to roll, using his body to keep the soldier pinned, his hand passed over where the Vietnamese's knife was sheathed. Grabbing the hilt of the knife and allowing the continued roll to withdraw it from its protection, he immediately changed the direction of the roll. As he rolled over his head, he had the knife turned outward so it would be thrust into the throat and jugular. When this happened he jerked his body slicing the airway and keeping any sound of alarm from escaping. Then he twisted once more sending the knife into the brain. The struggle was over.

He wasted no time. Turning the blade so he wouldn't cut himself, he rolled over to Mal, who instinctively had moved himself onto his side with his back facing Eddy. Back-to-back their bonds were where Eddy could cut Mal's. Once achieved, Mal returned the favor then cut Steve's.

They were free. They each gave an instant prayer of thanks that the others hadn't awakened.

"Never leave someone to sound the alarm or someone you might have to fight another day", he said to Mal. They both started quietly sneaking up on the sleeping gooks.

In an instant, both of the remaining guards were on their feet with their rifles trained on the three men. They had, in fact, been awaken and were only lying there, waiting.

Eddy turned to Mal and said, "We just have to stop thinking of these assholes as Viet Cong. They are North Vietnamese Regulars, trained and disciplined, not like their worthless counterparts in the South."

As they stood for what seemed an eternity wondering which group was the more scared, in less than a heart beat the wondering was over.

A figure detached itself from the shadows, wielding a knife that flashed in the firelight. One quick slice and blood spurted from the throat of one of the Vietnamese followed instantly by a thrust into the ear of the other.

As both silent corpses lay on the ground the Major stood over his handiwork.

It took years for Eddy to reconcile the turmoil of emotion that swept over him. One moment, he knew beyond any doubt that he was breathing his last breath on this earth, and the next he was feeling the greatest emotion of gratitude toward someone he thought was his enemy but had just saved their lives. His mind almost exploded. He literally didn't know what to do. Laugh or cry.

The Major helped him there. "Pitee! Pitee! OoHadeetyeh! PabyeJat! Da sveedanya!" The Major realized that the three Americans couldn't understand him, so he repeated himself in English. "Go! Go! Go away! Run! Go with God!

"Here", he continued. "These people, who will inherit the Earth, are not worth living. I thought you might try something tonight, so I stayed behind in case you needed help." Then looking down at the dead men he continued, "At first I didn't think you were going to. But, as it turns out, you did. They are a people without Honor. I only wish the Colonel were lying there with them. Here, take these." He threw a machete, an AK 47, and a couple of clips of ammunition at them, then turned and walked away.

Eddy thought as he watched him disappear into the jungle that there was a soldier. He hoped that the Major would find his way safely home, as well.

Then, without another second's delay, Eddy, Mal, and Steve picked up the weapons and took off into the jungle putting as much distance from the Colonel and his company as they could. Another long trek lay ahead but this was a flight to freedom.

Things seemed brighter. The three were exhausted but their steps were light. The weight of imprisonment had been lifted.

And they were ALIVE!!!!!

Chapter 9

WHERE THE ENERGY CAME FROM they didn't know. But, they ran -- and they ran -- and they ran. Streaking through the jungle at speeds that would make a competitor in Hawaii's Iron Man race give up and go home, they headed in as close to a southeasterly direction as they could maintain.

All they knew was they had to get as far from Nguyên as possible, and fast.

After a couple of hours of this relentless pace, they stopped. Exhausted beyond life and too weak to breathe, they rested.

Rest really is the wrong concept. For fugitives like these, there can be no rest. That is a luxury for stateside, not here. Each took a hundred-count, until they could breathe without it hurting, and then began searching the area for *sanctuary*, a place to hide and heal. A place they could at least take turns and sleep.

But, no such *safe harbor* could be found. So they went on, slower this time.

Running through the jungle at night is as close to crazy as they wanted to get. There are too many unseens. There weren't any little white lines to guide their way. To fly headlong into the dark was nuts. Anything could happen. Wouldn't it be ironic, to escape from Nguyên only to run full-blown into an American ambush and be killed? They wouldn't die from the bullets. They would have died from *stupidity*.

Slow down. Keep it easy. Conserve your strength. And, always, always head southeast. Who knows? Maybe they would run into the ocean.

The night sky lightened. The sun was touching the horizon. Tired, hungry, and extremely dehydrated from the vomiting and running, they stopped again. No real choice this time as they were standing at the base of a sheer cliff about a hundred and fifty feet tall.

Eddy ran his hand over his filthy hair and dog-eyed his companions. Steve stood woodenly while Mal squinted up at the rock wall facing them.

A ribbon of water ran along the base of the wall as far as they could see in either direction. The Earth, at some point in the millions and billions of years past, decided to change ground elevations abruptly. And, it did it right here. Could it possibly have happened when Earth's land was one continent called *Pangea*, before the tectonic plates decided to get a divorce and move away from each other? It's possible.

Steve remarked, "Family breakups are a bitch," as he stood there looking up and down the wall.

"I know," responded Mal instantly picking up the thought process. Spending as much time together as these guys did, they always knew what the other was thinking. "I hate it when that happens. That *Ground Up There* could have tried maybe one more time. Who knows? It could have all worked out."

"Then they would still be together, and we could just continue straight on instead of trying to find a way around," continued Steve. "Breakups always affect more than just the two involved.

"It was probably over some stray tree that just showed up wearing little or no bark and just dripping with sap."

"Oh, my God!" Mal jumped back in with feigned shocked. "Do y'all think the ground down here discovered a *rubber* tree, absent-mindedly left, discarded after a wild century of perverse grafting? Then, feeling rejected and betrayed, it packed the upper ground's rocks and shrubs, and told it to move out? The only problem was...the ground down here *kept* the stream."

"And, I suppose next you'll say," interjected Eddy not wanting to be left out of the fun and grateful for the American way of finding humor in the worst of circumstances, "the upper ground has to send monthly *stream support checks*. The ground down here can't be expected to take care of the stream alone. If the upper ground was interested enough to participate in the source conception, with all that disgusting and perverted movement before the upper ground got its *rocks* off, followed by the ejaculation of all that brown mud which was everywhere, then it damn sure can help with the burden of support."

Steve, Mal, and Eddy looked at each other in silence, each waiting for the other to break into laughter.

Steve was the first to speak. "We *are* a bunch of flipped-out psycho's. Time for the padded funny room." Then they experienced the all-encompassing tension release that can only come with laughter.

Eddy recognized humor and spirit. But, he also recognized when people had been pushed beyond exhaustion. Past the point, not where mistakes *could* be made, but *would* be made.

A mild form of this state is commonly called *overtired*. When little children experience this, they always do things that they know better than to do and end up getting into trouble. As adults, we regularly push ourselves in the daily struggle to just keep up achieving the same end.

We work too hard, or too long, and exhaust our minds and bodies. When this happens, for some totally unexplainable reason, we choose that moment to clean the house, or sit down and balance the check book, or most often we bring up and discuss some absolutely insignificant difference between us and whoever we are having a relationship with at the time, a subject that seems, in our weakened feebleness, to be the Armageddon of the total social and personal structure of our lives. Really important issues such as: *'Why do you always put your shoes in the closet toe first,'* or the infamous, *'You know, it wouldn't hurt to wipe down the shower door after you use it. I always have to do everything!'*

Eddy's favorite was the way we have to justify or explain the actions of others, as though any of us has control over any other person. We each have a full calendar taking care of ourselves.

'Why does your boss go out at night and party so much?'

'Well, you see. When I woke up this morning, God came and sat across the breakfast table from me. Much to my surprise, he appointed Your Husband the Keeper of his boss. So, what else was I to do? When I went to work, I put a

shotgun in his back and forced him into working seven days a week and twenty hours a day keeping the company that pays my salary in business, thereby putting a roof over our heads and food in our mouths. Then I made him, under pain of a merciless death, seek some personal recreation.

'He didn't want to. Honest! He argued and fought me the whole way!'

Eddy concluded that in his innocent years, before the war when he believed in God and the struggle between good and evil, the door to our soul for Satan to enter must surely be when we reach this exhaustive state.

It was time to stop and get some rest. They couldn't go on.

Scanning the cliff wall for a way over the top, he noticed a particularly dark area about thirty feet up and fifty yards from where they were standing.

"Let's check out this area to the right," he said to his two fellow escapees.

Staying in the stream, they walked to a spot just under the discoloration. Vines and roots were growing down the wall. Needing to get a closer look, Steve climbed up using the roots. This was not an easy task as the vines were too weak to hold his weight and the roots, which were strong enough, were covered with razor sharp thorns.

"I love this shit-hole Country!" Steve said examining the roots with all sarcasm intended.

He removed the rag he was using as a shirt. After tearing the shirt in half, he wrapped the two pieces around his hands. Digging his toes into any spot he could find to give himself a little extra push, he started the very slow climb.

His effort was rewarded. The spot turned out to be the small mouth of a cave that went back deep into the wall. The opening was only about four feet across. But, the smaller the better. The small opening made it easier to hide behind by moving the roots and vines, yet big enough to go through.

Considering their state of exhaustion, only the reward of rest could have given anyone the energy to climb that wall. With the extra incentive, they did.

No gift is totally free, Eddy realized.

As they crawled into the cave, Mal's nose picked up a smell, and it smelled really bad. In itself this wasn't unusual, as everything smelled bad. But this was different. It was dark and they couldn't make out any detail of what was toward the back.

On their walk, getting to their present location, they had each picked up a walking stick. Mal used his to prod forward into the cave, feeling his way. As he moved his stick, his eyes slowly adjusting to the dark and saw something move.

They froze. Silent.

Each closed his eyes speeding up the dilation of the iris. After about a thirty-count, Mal opened his and was staring at a den of fer-de-lance. *Ol' Two-Step*, was its nickname, another one of the great creations in this part of the world.

The Fer-de-lance is an extremely toxic, poisonous snake whose venom is hemotoxic. It hits the blood and destroys its oxygen carrying properties. It's called Ol' Two-Step because if it bites you, you will be dead in the time it takes to take *two steps*. Belonging to the viper family, it doesn't have the neurotoxic properties of the cobra. But, the volume of poison it pumps into its prey is enormous, a particularly nasty creature.

They weren't small, either. About four to five feet long and fat, about three and a half to four inches thick, musty dark upper bodies displaying the telltale diamond shape many people associate with rattlesnakes, with a light creamy yellow or green underbelly. Their coloring is especially dangerous as it gives them a natural camouflage, hiding them until it is too late. Their head is about the size of a grown man's fist, and they have the special ability to be able to open their mouth one hundred eighty degrees when they strike. They can get you anywhere.

Normally, they would have conceded the tenancy of this particular flat, what with rents being what they were and all, but exhaustion raised its ugly head.

The three started eviction procedures.

Chapter 10

THE IDEA OF HAVING TO contact the local Marshal's Office, paying them to serve the snakes a *Three Day to Pay or Quit* notice, and probably never catching the tenants at home before they could start legal proceedings, didn't really appeal to Eddy, so he took a more direct approach.

As best as they could count, there were about fifteen of the vipers. It was hard to tell because they were crawling around on top of one another. Or, would *slithering* be a better word? They didn't seem particularly interested in the three GIs. News probably hadn't gotten this deep into the jungle, as yet. Reptile correspondence is a bit slower than human.

Consider:

Some distant lizard hears about the landing of a group of Green Berets from the United States.

"Where's the United States?" it asks a passing snake.

"What isss a United Statessss?" responds the snake, then swallows the lizard.

A large bird, seeing the snake while circling above with intentions on the lizard, thinks the snake would be a much better meal for its family, so it swoops down to grab the snake with its talons before flying back to its home and hatchlings. A cat, hiding in a nearby bush that also had intentions on the lizard but didn't particularly find the snake appealing, changes its mind when the bird appears. Jumping on the bird before it can get more than a foot off of the ground, it bites down hard on the neck, snapping it. A passing dog sees the cat. The chase is on. As the cat ducks behind some wagons into an alley, the dog follows but is stopped short by an old Vietnamese woman who has already captured the cat and now grabs the dog. She proceeds to kill and skin both animals to prepare them for the evening meal. Her family arrives later and consumes the meal. Her son then goes out and joins his buddies who are weekend Viet Cong and raids the new American post. The raid is unsuccessful and the son is killed. His body lies unattended in the jungle to be consumed by the beetles that will later be eaten by a lizard.

A hell of a way to run a world.

Anyway, back to the eviction of the slithering drippy-teeth. Eddy knew that most animals only get up-tight if threatened. *What,* he wondered, *does a snake consider threatening? Better not to take a chance.*

The cave was very moist. The walls felt slimy. Nothing was dry enough to burn. Not to mention that a fire in the jungle from a raised height was like igniting a searchlight. Why not just take out an ad in the *Times* and announce their location? Better if there were no fires.

Guns made noise and they only had so many rounds of ammunition anyway.

"Whenever there is a dilemma," Eddy said, "always do the easiest thing." Steve used his walking stick to separate one snake from the rest. Then Mal used his stick to press down on the back of its neck long enough for Eddy to cut its head off with the machete.

"One down," counted Mal. Then the action was repeated until all were killed.

It didn't go completely smooth, of course. It never does. As the number of Fer-de-lance became fewer and the family-cuddle became not so cuddly, the snakes started to investigate what the hell was going on. As they came toward the guys, they had to be pushed back. This took at least one of the sticks, which meant both the separating and holding had to be done with the one remaining stick.

Mal mentioned that it was a good thing his grandmother hadn't been there. They might have escaped the snakes, but not one of the guys would have escaped having their mouths washed out with soap. Then again, Mal was convinced that God created profanity for situations like this.

Why else?

With the snakes dead and the heads disposed of, Eddy, Mal, and Steve settled back for a well-deserved sleep in the safety of their little jungle hide-a-way. Their sense of smell had adjusted to the stench to where it wasn't noticeable any longer. But of course, they did not sleep until they had gorged themselves, after expressing their gratitude for the best meal they had had since being taken captive.

They were, after all, Special Forces. And you know what they call the men who wear the Green Beret?

SNAKE EATERS!!!

Chapter **11**

There is a race of men that don't fit in.
A race that can't sit still,
So they break the heart of Kith and Kin,
And roam the world at will.

They seek the forest. They ford the glen.
They climb the mountain crest.
Theirs is the curse of the Gypsy's blood.
For they know not when to rest.

A poem by Robert Service

Chapter 12

EDDY'S SLEEP WAS DEEP, A sleep closer to death than any other living experience. But, the sleep was fitful, filled with nightmares. Even to the present day, he could remember them. It amazed him how much detail was still vivid.

In his dreams, one of the Fer-de-lance got away from the guys. It quickly slithered past Steve and Mal heading straight for Eddy. As it came to within a foot of his crouched body, it stopped. Coiling up and preparing to strike like a rattlesnake, which the Fer-de-lance does not do, it started to grow in size.

It grew and grew, getting larger and larger until it was as tall as he was, and it was still coiled. Frozen in place, Eddy couldn't move. He stood there holding the machete wondering why he hadn't used it. When the snake was smaller, he could have taken its head off with one stroke, but at this size it would only piss it off.

The snake and Eddy just froze, looking at each other. Steve and Mal, in Eddy's dream, didn't even notice or react, as though the snake was invisible. They just kept hacking away at the normal ones.

Where did they get the second machete? Eddy wondered, and then realized that anything was possible in a dream.

"Hey, guys!" Eddy called to them. "Mind giving me a hand here?"

They never even turned around. It was as though Eddy were invisible, too.

"OK!" he said looking back directly into the snake's eyes. "It's just you and me. Don't ask me how those two can miss seeing a snake that's over thirty feet long and a couple of feet thick... But, hell the what!" Once again he reversed his words.

The snake didn't answer back. They both just stayed there staring at one another with the snake's tongue darting in and out, tasting the air. They stared deeply into each other's eyes.

Suddenly, the snake's head, which was about three feet across and at this size more resembled a dragon than a snake, started to have large bumps appear then disappear all over it. The head would swell-out with a tumor for a moment, and then the tumor would recede back to normal. It would repeat the action on a different part of its head. Then again and again.

The snout started to recede, becoming blunt instead of pointed. The tongue continued to move in and out picking up Eddy's fear.

In amazed disbelief, Eddy slowly lowered the machete from the position he had it, ready to strike a futile blow if the snake came any closer.

Then the snake did something that blew Eddy's mind. As its snout was getting smaller and the pulsating and swelling increased in speed and frequency it lifted up its head staring at the ceiling of the cave. It then opened its mouth and let out a bloodcurdling human scream. It kept screaming as it started to sway back and forth. The swaying got faster and more violent. The scream -- deafening.

Eddy, stepping back, stumbled on something and fell down against the cave wall.

No means of retreat.

Cornered!

He just sat there watching this convulsion of Hell.

Just as fast as the screaming started, it stopped.

Silence.

The snake lowered its head and once again stared at Eddy. Only now it wasn't the snake's face he saw, but Nguyên's.

72

The goddamn snake had Nguyên's head on it, and it was not three feet in front of him, tongue darting in and out, Nguyên's face with a snake's tongue.

Eddy struck. No thinking first, just pure reaction.

He looked down at the blood on the machete then at the severed head that rolled against the cave wall. As the head came to a stop, the eyes opened and it spoke to Eddy in a hollow disconnected voice unmistakably Nguyên's.

"You're weak. We will inherit the Earth." Then its eyes closed and it was silent.

Eddy thought, *This is a bitch of a nightmare!*

Chapter 13

THE JUNGLE IS IMMENSE IN ITS CONFINEMENT. Eddy realized that that saying was an *oxymoron,* a self-contradicting statement, like *Military Intelligence.* But, it nevertheless was true. On their trek to freedom, Eddy, Mal, and Steve began accepting the size of the land. Many evenings, when they stopped to rest, the conversations alluded to this.

They had given up the idea of traveling at night and resting during the day about a week before. The progress had been too slow, and the terrain way too treacherous. Steve had suffered multiple lacerations on his left hand that for a long time didn't seem to want to stop bleeding.

Viet Nam has a native botanical system only equaled by the rain forests of the South American Amazon. Strange and exotic plants grow in great profusion. Most of these are not designed for the betterment of man. In fact, it is just the opposite. Such was the case of one particular type of tree and its relationship with Steve.

The tree itself is not dangerous. Its leaves, bark, sap, and pulps are not poisonous. Monkeys, birds, and insects all found a home in its foliage. Because many of the non-human natives of this biosphere preferred this particular tree as its haven was the first indication that it meant trouble for those creatures inhabiting the ground. Man being one.

The base of the trunk stops about three to five feet above the ground. The roots sprout out and go into the soil searching for the needed water and nutrients to sustain its life. The tree is large, probably a mutation of a banyan tree. The trunks grow anywhere up to eight feet across. The roots begin at the trunk with a diameter averaging six to eight inches and slowly taper down as they reach the ground.

Not being a botanist, Eddy conjectured that the reason the root system didn't start at ground level was that so much moisture was available above the ground. Over the course of the multiple millennia of evolution the roots slowly became more and more exposed.

You may say, 'Yeah, but...water isn't the only sustaining element a tree needs.' And, you would be right. Hence the reason Steve's hand looked like it had gotten caught in a spaghetti-making machine.

The exposed roots are covered by razor sharp thorns, which vary in size from an inch to a tiny little bud. Only, as the thorn tapered to its point, it also sharpened. This would create a real deterrent for any ground animal trying to climb up to attack its upper level inhabitants, a true symbiotic relationship.

Well, these benefits to the monkeys and birds Steve didn't find really all that beneficial.

The constant rains cause the jungle floor to be saturated. In other words, mud. As the three escapees were going down a particular embankment, which sloped at a forty to forty-five degree angle for about fifty feet, the mud gave way under Steve's boots and he slipped. This happened constantly and it wasn't particularly alarming. Add to the dilemma that it was night and darker than Nguyên's heart, Steve's expletive; "Oh, shit!!" had a downward inflection at the end. More like a statement than the upward inflection of a question or a frightened alarm.

But, natural human reactions sometime take over. Reactions we don't consciously think of. The body just does them.

In this case, the reaction was to reach out and find something to grab on to preventing the uncontrolled slide down the hill. The human mind has a real problem with the sensation of falling.

By this point, it shouldn't take a nuclear physicist to figure out what Steve's hand found to grab.

Steve emitted a second expletive. Only this one had the very definite upward deflection known to all of us that have experienced sudden unexpected pain, kind of like slipping off of the bicycle pedal -- only sharper.

Steve's slide continued, slicing the skin.

When Eddy and Mal got to the bottom of the incline, Steve was grabbing his left wrist, cutting off the blood-flow to the hand. He later mentioned that he was happy to have been the benefactor of the extra nutrients needed by the tree, but right then and there, the tree and its nutrients could go screw themselves.

"God! I hate this country!" he snarled.

Tearing his own shirt to make a bandage, Mal grabbed some leaves from the jungle floor and put them on Steve's hand before wrapping it with the cloth. A cloth will soak up blood, but water-saturated leaves seal the wound, keeping the blood in, rather than causing blood to be drawn out. They'd have to worry about bacteria later.

Eddy wished he could have found something that would seal off Steve's pain. But, such is the nature of misfortune.

Chapter 14

Cussing at the country and looking at his hand wrapped in the rag, Steve joined Eddy and Mal as they continued on. There was no way of telling how far they had come. No maps. No signs stating the distance to the next off-ramp or town, only the constant jungle.

The jungle just went on and on. Yet, at times it would seem to close in around them like prison walls. It didn't seem to matter if the terrain went up or down. The Central Highlands were named appropriately. They were in the middle of the country if you included the North and South together, and they were mountainous.

Not mountains as would be thought comparing them with the Rockies or the High Sierras, but compared to the flat swamp-like marshland of the Delta, mountains, never the less. If you didn't think so, try walking across them.

You could ascend five or six hundred feet or more only to walk back down the same distance on the other side. But, the jungle never changed.

The trees in the valleys would sometimes grow taller than the ones on the mountaintops, each trying to compete with the other for the precious sunlight above the canopy. When one flies over the mountains, this effect gives the illusion that they are not as steep or severe as they actually are. The canopy levels everything out in its lush green splendor. From the air, the country was actually quite beautiful, a total contrast to one's opinion of it on the ground.

The land sucked!

On and on the three walked. There was no hurry. No plane to catch or schedule to keep. It was better to be slow and cautious than fast and foolish. Steve was living proof.

As the days and nights passed, the duty of obtaining food fell on Eddy and Mal more and more. Steve's hand continued to give him pain. The body's ability to numb-out had helped, but the pain had taken its toll and it seemed to be getting worse.

Dining al fresco may be a sought-after delight in the European countryside or as a means of diversion for the spoiled rich, but to Eddy, Mal, and Steve, it was a fact of staying alive.

Knowing they couldn't hunt using a rifle, (the noise would alert possibly the wrong people as to their presence) they called upon their intense training in survival. Quite fortunately, the most versatile plant in the world is bamboo, and Viet Nam is more than generous with its supply.

It sometimes grows so thick it completely blocks out the sunlight causing total darkness. These areas are impossible to navigate. You have to go around. There is no choice. Most bamboo forests are not made up of stalks about one or two inches thick as we are used to seeing at home. Eddy remembered them sometimes six inches in diameter and twenty to thirty feet tall. You couldn't cut them down. They had to be blown down with explosives.

But clearing out bamboo was not a concern. They were grateful for its existence. Further gratitude was given up that the Major had thrown them the machete. It had become more useful than the rifles, which they hadn't used and hoped they wouldn't have to.

Bamboo can be made into many things. The stalks, being a grass, were stringy. You could strip them, then by keeping the strands wet, tie or weave them into strong lines or ropes depending on the thickness you wanted. Cut thicker, the stalks were flexible, yet resilient. That aspect, used with a little ingenuity, know-how, and direct stealing of the design from the Montagnards who had been doing it for centuries, a very accurate and very silent crossbow could be fashioned. This is what Bai Son taught Eddy and it became the saving grace for the three fugitives.

Up until the time they made the crossbow, the mainstay of food consisted of fruits growing wild in the jungle, grubs, insects, and of course the Fer-de-lance.

You had to be careful with the fruit. Some were poisonous. As a general rule, if a plant emits a white liquid when the stem or branch is broken, don't eat it. The best tasting fruit was one that looked and tasted like a kiwi. Only, it wasn't oval. It had five ridges running the length of its two inches. If cut in half, width wise, the two halves looked like a five pointed star. Its taste was sweeter than a kiwi. Whenever the guys found any of these, the trees were stripped.

Many days passed where there was no food at all. Water was plentiful. All this country did was rain. When the rain came down the three drank their fill from large leaves they used to catch the descending *life-blood*. But, good water was another matter. Between the rotting plant life on the floor of the jungle and the dead animals that abound, being rapidly consumed by the carrion beetles, when it wasn't raining standing water turned bad very quickly.

Funny thing about being a fugitive from a POW situation: Nobody hands out halazone or iodine tablets so you can purify the water you find. Many times Eddy and the guys had to drink from mud puddles. Whatever was in the water, besides hydrogen and oxygen, just had to stay in the water. There was nothing they could do about it. If they ended up fighting some intestinal parasite, so be it. At least they would be alive to fight the parasite, rather than dead from dehydration.

There was a time when the only thing they found to eat was the ever-present leech. Somehow, none of the guys could bring themselves to try one of these vampires of the jungle floor.

If not a leech, how about a "Little Red Piss Ant?"

Now here was a really charming character of Creation. Eddy knew if there was a God, he had passed on this one. It was created from the *Bowels of Hell*. No question about it!

Most ants can be eaten. In many parts of the world they are considered a delicacy. But, these little...!

They are vicious. While not being necessarily big, about the size of a common red ant, they more than make up for it in aggression. If someone brushed the leaves of a plant they occupy, they run out to the furthest leaf and stand up on their back four legs, lifting the front two and the head which supported huge open mandibles, in total defiance. The size or character of the *enemy* didn't matter.

Eddy remembered when he was first told about these things. They were walking through a rubber plantation, a favorite home for the ants, and a seasoned sergeant pointed them out.

The sergeant brushed the plant. Then, as the ant ran out to the end challenging its enemy who was millions of times bigger, the sergeant held a lit cigarette, burning end first, toward the ant. Almost every creature, big or small, runs from fire. Not these guys. With mandibles pinching, it leaped onto the lit end and held on, cremating itself in the process.

Sometimes you wouldn't detect them getting on you. Eddy remembered one hapless soldier walking through a rubber plantation near the trees. He suddenly screamed in pain and started jumping up and down, cussing and screaming. Seemingly for no reason, he started to swat at his crotch, thrashing about as though he were possessed.

He pulled his pants down. And there, on the head of his pecker, was a little red piss ant with his mandibles buried deep into the tender flesh.

Everyone busted up laughing. But the poor GI who was the victim, somehow missed the humor in the whole thing. It wasn't a goddamn bit funny to him.

Eat little red piss ants? Eddy didn't think so!

Once they had made a couple of crossbows, and after a bit of practice, they were able to shoot small animals. These were rare but welcomed. The jungle, as an animal habitat, doesn't just sit there and let you attack it. Animals know you're coming before you do. They hide. Most of the kills were accomplished near a watering hole that had a lot of small footprints around it.

There, they would lie in wait for the creatures to show up. When the animal started to drink, -- sssssT! Skewered!

Animal paths were also good. Over tens of thousands of years, animals going from one place to another on the jungle floor would always take the same route. Eventually a path would be worn. The jungle had a voracious habit of growing back and covering up what had been there the day before. But, as the millennia passed, even the stubborn jungle learns. The plants grow the other way.

A perfect example of the growing hunger of the foliage was the futility of *Agent Orange.*

The most dangerous problem with moving troops on roads through the jungle in Viet Nam, was that the jungle itself grew right up to the edge of the road. And it was dense. This created a perfect place for Charlie to hide waiting to ambush a passing column.

So, some scientific genius back stateside came up with this chemical defoliant called Agent Orange, due to its bright orange color. When sprayed over the plant life growing along the roadside, every living organism died. This helped prevent ambushes by pushing back the jungle a couple of hundred feet from the road on both sides.

It did, however, have a couple of problems.

The jungle, in its very nature, doesn't like to be pushed back. So it simply grew back in a week to where it was just as thick as before. This required more spraying.

Secondly, the scientists, in their rush to create a product usable and marketable to the government, and the government, who historically look to the short solution while ignoring the long-term results thereby creating an instant source of wealth, didn't give a damn. They didn't bother to take the time to test the effect this chemical had on the human bodies that passed through it every day.

Many GIs were killed in Viet Nam from many sources. Those killed by Agent Orange simply didn't know it until years later at home, slowly being eaten up by cancer.

Eddy hoped that the scientists were forced into not taking the time to test. He hoped that they didn't know. He hoped the chemical company owners and stockholders didn't know. He hoped that his government fathers, who asked him to go to war to fight for a cause he didn't understand but had been raised to depend on them to understand, didn't know.

He hoped!

If they knew -- and did it anyway?

The answer to this question was best left unanswered. It was a question with no good result. A question only history could judge. And history had a way of being a strict schoolmaster.

On another note, Eddy thought back to the types of food they ate on their trek, and some of the tastes. It wasn't like when he was at a particular Base Camp, where C Rations and K Rations were choppered in on a periodic basis. One place that stood out in his memory was Bunker Hill. So named because it was on the top of a mountain and was covered with bunkers. His unit had been there for quite a few months and it acted as a base of operation for the area. When the unit first arrived the mountaintop was covered with trees. The first job was to clear off the entire top so it was as bare as a baby's ass. One-O-Five millimeter howitzers were to be brought in by chopper and bunkers were to be dug in. Until the foliage was cleared, none of the previous could be done. It required chopping, digging, and burning. Eventually a bulldozer was used because the bamboo was so thick. It had to be blown down, pushed away, and then burned to ashes.

While they were there, Eddy got a *care package* from his mother. Care packages were packages shipped to troops overseas. Viet Nam is overseas, and Eddy was a troop. His mom was a well intending single woman who knew nothing of how the Army ships material. The package contained two bottles of wine, which was very welcomed as none was available to troops in the boonies, canned vegetables, sent because Eddy had mentioned in a letter that everything over there was green except the vegetables, toilet paper, another response to a complaint, books, writing paper and pens, and two large loaves of bread. The last was the most memorable.

Eddy's mom didn't realize that all care packages came over by ship. The time it took a shipment to get to Viet Nam was one solid month. The bread was carefully wrapped in aluminum foil to preserve its freshness. You can wrap a loaf in gold if you want, but a month in a damp, humid, ship's storage area does something to the bread.

When Eddy, Mal, and Steve went to unwrap the bread, excited about finally getting something not out of a can, as the foil was opened a puff of blue powder rose from the middle. The entire loaf had molded to the point of being nothing but a spider web of mold fibers wrapped in foil in the shape of a loaf of bread.

The three laughed about that for weeks.

On the top of a mountain across a particularly large valley was another Base Camp named Brillo Pad because of its shape being like a squished steel wool pad of the same name.

Both bases operated in their own territories and worked together with admirable cooperation. One time Brillo Pad got attacked and Eddy, on Bunker Hill, called in an air strike on the location as requested by the commanding officer of Brillo Pad due to his view from afar. The air strike came after a failed attempt to use a new, highly classified artillery round called a COFRAM. It was made for the 155mm and 8-inch Howitzer. The round was especially nasty to any ground personnel exposed in the open. Each shell ejected fifty butterfly bombs, that sprouted spring loaded wings, out of the base of the round about 500 feet above the target. As the bombs spun downward they struck the ground on a trigger on the base that fired a round grenade fifteen feet in the air where it exploded into thousands of metal ball bearings. This had the effect of blowing a multitude of holes in anything they came in contact with – especial human bodies.

The problem was one had never been called for in battle. Eddy, seeing the human wave attack taking place on the adjacent hill top, call for the round. Well, the trajectory was computed, like normal, at the artillery firebase. Then, due to the classified and untried nature of the piece, the trajectory had to be recomputed at Battalion level, then Division, then Army. By the time the first round was fired it was three and a half hours after Eddy called for the mission.

And of course, it was so far off target, Eddy couldn't even see the explosions.

"Fuck it," said Eddy over the radio. "Substitute Hotel-Echo (High Explosive) and go back to original coordinates. Fire for effect.

"Blue boy. Are you up there?"

"Hear you loud and clear," came the reply from the Air Force spotter plane pilot.

"Mark the Willy-Peter (White Phosphorus round) and bring in the big boys."

"Roger."

"Break," continued Eddy. "Bravo 5. Give me one shot Willy Peter for the Blue Boys."

"Roger," came the reply. "You got it.

"By the way, Bravo 46, I was told to tell you to watch your language on the air."

"Wilco that," replied Eddy. "Wouldn't want Charlie to think we were a bunch of uncouth, foul-mouth bastards. They might not understand when we fuck-up their little attack."

"Roger, Bravo 46. Fire over."

"Fire out."

After the White Phosphorus round hit, Eddy was back on the horn. "Bravo 5. Drop Five-Zero, fire for effect."

The strike was successful and the attack was thwarted. Comes in handy to have *Big Brother next door.*

Much to the delight of the GIs on Bunker Hill, when they were supplied, along with the rations they would receive, beer and soda would also be brought in by sling-load. These treats, along with the mail, were the high-point in the combat soldier's day. The beer and soda were warm and they were drunk that way. So what. A very small sacrifice for such a heavenly treat.

This was not the case in their survival trek to freedom. They ate almost anything, and nothing was delivered, especially beer and soda.

He understood why primates survived more than most species. Monkey tastes terrible! It was tough, stringy, and bitter. Insects and grubs were more succulent.

Eddy laughed to himself. Many times, once he got back stateside when he would go to a nice restaurant with a girl hoping to impress her enough to allow the evening to progress past the dinner stage, he would order oysters on the half shell or escargot. When the girl would make some comment like, "God! How can you eat that? I'd starve first," he would break into laughter and lose control. He instantly stopped caring whether he impressed her or not, let alone worry about Bò-kò Boom-Boom.

"You are so spoiled!" he would begin. "You don't know what you're talking about. You've never gone hungry a day in your over-protected life. What do you know about starving? What do you know about being hungry? What do you know about what you would or would not eat? In fact, what do you know about anything?!!"

Then he would stand up and storm out of the restaurant, leaving her there.

Eddy did have a problem dating the same girl more than once.

He remembered the constant ordeal of obtaining food, such as the time he and Mal were next to an animal trail waiting for that night's dinner to come along. They were hidden from view and up-wind, so the unsuspecting prey couldn't get a whiff of their scent.

Not that any self-respecting animal would want to, of course. By this time, Eddy knew they had to be pretty ripe. It had been weeks since they had last bathed, and that was accomplished by walking across a small river. Not the cleanest source of water they could have found.

As they were hidden with their crossbows at the ready, they heard a slight disturbance in the brush. Something was approaching their position. They were on the alert as the sound got closer. Whatever it was was pretty good sized. This might be a meal for a couple of days or so. They didn't want to miss it. Eddy was hoping it was a boar or something equal to it.

As he was sighting down the shaft of the arrow laid across the top of the crossbow, he suddenly realized he was looking at a full-grown tiger.

A crossbow arrow hitting a full-grown tiger would be like expecting a straight pin to take down a pit-bull with an attitude. More than likely, it would just piss him off!

Luckily, they were hidden. But, for how long they didn't know. They had to do something to get rid of it.

Couldn't stand up and yell. That would present the tiger with its evening meal, which, if you asked Eddy and Mal in confidence, was not the plan of the day.

So, what to do?

Eddy had an idea. He slowly signaled Mal. Both were ready.

Eddy shot an arrow into the jungle past the tiger, just missing its nose. The beast's first reaction was to stop and stare in the direction the arrow went to see what had flown past its nose so fast. Then it slowly moved in the direction of the flight, sniffing cautiously.

When it was turned with its tail toward the guys, Mal fired an arrow right up its ass.

The tiger jumped about six feet into the air and let go with a deafening roar! When it came down, it turned in the direction of its pain. SsssT! Another arrow, sticking into a rear paw, followed by another into its front.

Every time it got hit by one of the arrows it turned in that direction thinking it was being attacked on all sides by some invisible beast that stung. Finally it couldn't take anymore and just ran off the way it came. After it had gone, the two bravely laughed like hell.

But, *only after it* had gone.

Eddy grinned at Mal, "Tiger meat probably tastes like shit, anyways."

"I'll bet it tastes like slow natives," responded Mal.

"Cute."

Chapter 15

TIME PASSED, WHETHER SLOWLY OR in an instant it passed. The same with the mountains under their feet. Both became a blur to the three. How far had they traveled? How many days had come and gone? The guys didn't know and they didn't care.

At some point in their trek, Mal woke up in the morning and announced that his birthday was around this time of year. Had it been yesterday? Was it today? Tomorrow? A week from whenever? They just didn't know. Eddy and Steve sang *Happy Birthday*. Everyone knew what his birthday wish was. They didn't have to ask.

"How did you grow up, Mal?" asked Steve.

"Same way most people from the South do, I suppose," answered the Sergeant. "I grew up on a farm. Most folks in my neck of the woods are farmers. My dad was also the local preacher. We were Baptists, but since ours was the only church around, my pa would sometimes throw in a word or two for the Methodists. I never really understood the difference. Baptists *dip*, and Methodists *sprinkle*. Big difference.

"But, preach'n don't pay much so we had to farm. We had a few cows, horses, chickens, ducks, pigs, and a lot of tobacco. Tobacco was the major source of income for my family, as much as it was. We weren't rich, but we had all we needed. There was a swimming hole to dive in or swing over from the rope tied to a tree that my grandpa hung when he was a kid that went over the edge. This was done usually in the summer. The winters were too damn cold to go jumping in a pond.

"There were streams, and rivers to fish in. My dog, Ol' Bogey, and I would spend many hours on the bank with my cane rod stabbed into the soft soil and the line with a cork on the end bobbling in the water. I loved to fish. I honestly didn't care if I caught anything or not. Laying back with my hands under my head, with Ol' Bogey lying next to me, I allowed the sun to soak away all my troubles. Believe me, that was the life."

"Did you go to school?" asked Steve. "This sounds like you were the embodiment of Huck Finn. Did you suck on a piece of straw as you laid there by the river?"

"You bet I did. Nothing better'n this, or any other world. And yes. I went to school. Never graduated from high school. Too much to do around the farm to be worrying about no education. Plus, Dad did a lot of home schooling. I learned to read by reading The Good Book. I had no dreams or desire to go to college. A farmer don't need no degree to slop hogs or plant and pick tobacco, and I certainly didn't have the calling to become no Preacher Man.

"No. I may not be the most educated man in the world, but no one had a better life. I'm going back to it when we get home from this mess. I'm going back to the bank of that river. I'm going to take my old rod, may not even put a worm on the hook. Ol' Bogey died a couple of years ago. He was fifteen. The best dog a man could ever wish for. I'm going to get another Golden pup. I'll name it Li'l Bogey. The two of us will have a great life."

"What about girls?" asked Eddy.

"Oh. I had a slew of them," responded Mal. "I'm a bit of a stud, you know. Yep. Girls weren't a problem. I may be the son of a Preacher, but I was a bit wild. I guess most Preacher's children are. Did a bit of skinny-dipping in the ol' swimming hole. The problem was deciding which girl."

"You don't have a special one?" asked Steve, the married *match-maker*.

"Not really. Although, there is this one; Beverley Jean. Now there is one kick-ass woman. She's not only pretty, but she is a spitfire. She don't take nothin' off of nobody. I really like her. Just might marry her when I get back. That is, if no one else has grabbed her up. Didn't feel right about tying her down while I was at war.

"I know, Steve. Y'all feel different. And that's OK for you and Linda. But I just couldn't do it. Besides, maybe she's changed while I've been gone playing Army. Maybe she's not the girl she used to be."

"Maybe you're not the man *you* used to be, either," said Steve.

"Maybe not. But that's my point. I just thought it would be better to wait. That's all.

"How'd you end up in the Army?" asked Eddy.

"Volunteered. Wanted to get out of Thibodaux, Louisiana, and experience the world. My Grandpa was with Patton in World War II. My Pa was in Korea with MacArthur. It was just something I was raised to know I had to do. When I became of age, my Grandpa, Pa, and I sat down and looked at all the possibilities and decided on the Army. Once that decision was made it only seemed the right thing to do to go all the way. So, here I am; stuck with you two Yankees eating grubs and snake. I probably should have given it a little more thought.

"What about you, Steve? We know you're married, but what about your life and childhood? I just gave an account of mine, now what about yours?"

"Mine's kind of boring, actually," replied Steve. "I graduated from high school in Rochester, New York, after spending the last four years on the swim and track teams. I love distance running and always had ambitions of becoming a marathoner, or maybe going for the Iron Man. I love biking as well, and was good at it. I competed in a few triathlons and it seemed to be a good fit. I placed in the top ten in some of the local races, but never had the opportunity for the big races. I got my draft notice during the year I took off from school to run. I was planning on going to college, but Johnson had other ideas. I never did like that guy.

"Anyway. I was working at Sears in the shoe department to make enough money to support myself. I moved out of my parents' home after high school and rented a small apartment with a buddy from school who I could trust to carry his part of the burden. It was a good year — until I got the notice. I didn't want to be drafted and get thrown into the infantry, so I joined and signed up for communication. The opportunity came to get into this outfit, so I took it."

"When did you meet Linda?" asked Mal.

"I was home on leave, after finishing my Black Ops training, when my dad invited me out to dinner with one of his business associates. At the dinner were his wife and two kids: a son and daughter. The son was a freshman in high school and a pretty good guy. The daughter...well... How can I say this right? She was knock-dead gorgeous. And smart, too. She bowled me over right from the start."

"It was Linda, wasn't it?" asked Mal.

"Yep! And I was gone. I never stood a chance. We started dating and decided within the month that we were destined to be together for the rest of our lives. On my next leave, before coming over here, we got married. I have never, and will never, regret that choice.

"We talked a lot about the possibilities that laid ahead of us, and none of them mattered. We both honestly agreed that we'd rather spend one day together, than a lifetime without the other.

"Mal, if you marry Beverley Jean when you get home, you'll understand what I mean. Finding that *soul-mate,* the one person you can be yourself around, the person who knows you better than you know yourself, the person who knows the worst things about you, and it's OK. That is the person with whom you don't even question your future.

"I'm going to make it home. I know I will. And I'll do it because of Linda. She is my driving force and the reason to live. Now, it's up to you too idiots to insure that will happen. Let's get this show on the road. We've spent enough time talking about things that don't matter right now."

"You're wrong, Steve," said Eddy. "These things do matter. They matter most. What we are doing isn't a walk in the park. It's harder than any marathon. The motivation to see it through is what's truly important. Without it, anyone would have given up long before now."

"Spoken like a Yankee College boy who's so full of shit he can't see from daylight," broke in Mal. Y'all 're right, but you're still full of shit.

"Let's go."

The march to freedom continued.

Days couldn't be counted because they didn't know for sure when one started or stopped. Many times, due to exhaustion, they would stop and rest in the daytime. Falling asleep, time passed undetected. How much? Did they sleep until the next day, or just a couple of hours? They weren't sure. They stopped standing watch. They just prayed that they would be left alone, and so far the prayers had been answered.

Eddy supposed if it had been important, they would have found a way of keeping track of time. All he cared about was the morale of the three. The biggest macho asshole in the world can be brought to his knees by exhaustion and lack of proper nutritional sustenance. The guys were showing the strain.

At first it displayed itself as anger, little petty squabbles over really insignificant things. Sometimes, days would go by where one wouldn't speak to another because he missed a bird with the crossbow causing them to settle for eating grubs. The arguments were usually between Eddy and Mal. Steve, as the time passed, got more lethargic... almost Zombie-like.

His hand was looking bad. The bleeding had stopped, but the cuts weren't closing. The skin was turning a strange color. Eddy didn't like the looks of it at all.

Exhaustion even takes its toll on exhaustion. Too tired to fight with each other and brought to the point where they just didn't care anymore, quietness fell over the three.

Gone were the intimacies. Gone were the friendly talks where they would compare notes on their women at home.

The longer a guy was in country the more he got used to the idea that he wasn't going home alive, and neither were his buddies. It was a strange sensation knowing you're going to die. You just didn't know when.

Soldiers in Viet Nam consisted of two social attitudes. One type would spend his whole tour alone. He didn't want to get to know anybody. This was usually a guy who got into a bad firefight soon after arriving, where a lot of men are killed. It hurt to see a friend die. So, the best solution to keep from hurting was to have no friends. Then when people around you were killed you felt bad, but it didn't hurt the same way.

The second is the guy who wants to know everything about you. He's not being nosy. He is honestly interested. This type believes that a person's life will go on after death if their memories are passed to another. They share everything.

Eddy, Mal, and Steve were all of the second variety. They knew more about each other than their own mothers did. Some conversations involved their various experiences with the fairer sex. They were never intended to demean women. On the contrary. They were light-hearted stories shared to keep themselves from going insane.

Every combat soldier realized very quickly that they had to keep a strong hold on what they were, hopefully, going home to. If that hold came in the form of a tale involving sex, so be it. These three respected the opposite sex more than most. In actuality, it was more of a *compliment,* than a *put-down.*

One time, before his hand got shredded, Steve was *bragging* about the beauty of his wife and how they loved to partake in long sessions of lovemaking in various locations. Many times it was her idea.

"This one time," he began.

"Oh, not again!" broke in Eddy. "Goddamnit, Steve! Every time you start telling me about Linda's prowess, I start thinking that I'm going to spend the rest of my life wishing for *her.* No woman loves it *that* much!"

"Maybe some women have a bigger appetite than your little *snack* can provide," Steve responded, one up on Eddy. "Anyway, Linda and I were in the mountains in Vermont where we went for a short hike. I was in the lead and was concentrating on the trail so much I didn't notice that she slowly dropped back and had ducked behind a tree.

"I turned to say something to her and she wasn't there. I called out. No answer. Well, this vixen has a sense of humor, so anything was possible. I thought she probably crept ahead on the trail and was waiting in ambush to jump out and scare the shit out of me. So, I got off the trail, and quietly moved forward. As I went... "

"Is this going to take all day," broke in Mal. "Or, are you going to get to the point?"

"What's your rush?" responded Steve. "You got a plane to catch to the local cathouse down there in the Bayou of (with a full mock-Southern drawl) Laweezeeaanah? Some Southern honey need your *manhood* to remind her how good the Yanks were in school, and why the South lost the War?"

"Don't you go off on the Confederacy. I'll kick your Yankee ass all the way to hell and back. I will!"

Eddy knew all this was done with humor, so he didn't try to break it up. They were the best of friends and would die for each other.

If someone else had said that stuff to Mal, it would have been Steve doing the kicking. You didn't mess with any one of these three, or the other two would mess with you. But, to each other, they were brutal.

"Anyhow. Before I was so rudely interrupted by my *inbred* friend...."

"Watch what you say about my Mama. She and Uncle Clem loved each other. Anyways, my Daddy wasn't very well endowed. At least, that's what Sis said."

That brought laughter to all of them, a bit too loudly for their situation. It took every ounce of strength they had to keep from screaming. Eddy and Steve fell on the ground holding their sides, trying to keep quiet while their ribs convulsed in pain.

Finally catching his breath and not wanting to be outdone by no Johnny Reb, Steve continued. "Anyway. I moved ahead..."

"Jesus Christ!" Eddy broke in this time. "You aren't going to stop, are you?"

"Nope!"

"Well then, we might as well let him finish or this will take all day."

"Go for it, Dickhead!" agreed Mal.

"So, anyway. I crept forward hearing a small noise. I crouched down and crawled slowly from tree to tree. I was determined to turn her little surprise around. As I crawled around this one tree, there, in a small clearing about fifteen feet across, lying spread-eagle, right in the middle -- was Linda. Naked as the day she was born, but a whole lot prettier. Her hands were outstretched, beckoning me.

"'Come here, Stud. Take me, now! Or, you'll lose me forever,' she said.

"Well. I didn't need a second invitation. She had me more than satisfied in less time than you have intelligence, Mal."

"I've heard that about you," responded Mal, always wanting to get the last word. "No staying power. One pump, and POW! You're done. Too bad. Maybe when we get home, I'll just have to come up there to Rochester, New York and visit. Then Linda can find out what a real man is like. Of course, she won't be worth anything to you afterwards. She'll never be satisfied with a Damn Yank again.

"Just promise me that you'll be kind to her after my visit. If she tries to be nice to you and, even though she knows she's in for a disappointment, performs her wifely *duty* and while she's on top, she suddenly kicks her heals like she's wearing spurs, and waves one arm over her head letting out a Rebel Yell, know that it's just a flashback. Don't take it personally."

"Hey!" interrupted Eddy, wanting to be part of the fun. "Have you been to California, Mal? I dated a girl that did just that. Like she was riding a bucking bronco."

"California?" exclaimed Mal. "Hell no! Why would I want to go to California? Only thing there are hot-rodders and queers. Say -- never noticed it before, but I don't see no steering wheel on you. Better watch it, Steve. Maybe you and I should take turns on watch. Charlie may not be the only thing that goes *bump* in the night."

"Get screwed!" responded Eddy.

"See!" continued Mal. "Now he's openly offering. Thanks Eddy, but no thanks. You're not my type. Besides, the Army stuck it to me enough. I'm pretty much taken care of. Thanks for the offer, anyway."

With that, they all gave each other a pat on the shoulder, sanity firmly in place, got up and continued their trek.

Girlfriends and wives would be really upset and not very understanding if they knew how the guys talked over there. Divulging intimacies. Openly discussing their sex lives. Discussing everything, including their periods and how they dealt with bouncing hormones. But, Eddy knew: Immortality had been achieved. They would live forever. If not on this earth, they would live in each other's hearts.

The sixties was a period of open sex: Free love, and all that. But down deep nothing really changes. A person respects another person, or they don't. It doesn't matter what morays society deems as acceptable. These three respected all others, except maybe the Vietnamese. And that was for a good reason.

After walking a few minutes, Mal asked. "Say, Steve? Do you have a picture of Linda?"

"I did," responded Steve, "until that Nguyên took it."

"No. Not that one. I saw that one. I mean a naked picture."

"What?! Hell no."

"You want to buy one?"

So ended another day on their march to freedom. No woman will ever understand the real meaning of camaraderie. Women talk about *respect*. There is no greater respect one can have for another than knowing their most intimate secrets are safe. Many marriages ended because the returning GI tried to find that same comfort zone in their spouse. But, the wives just didn't get it.

Steve's marriage came to an early end. But, as the rainwater dripped from his nose in the present day, Eddy remembered, it wasn't because of sexual dissatisfaction.

Thinking back to that day of laughter, and the slowly degenerating weeks that followed, the laughter seemed eons ago. The humor left them. Their steps became heavy. The humidity was ridiculous, their energy level low. Mistakes were being made. At first it was little things, like the aforementioned missing of game with the crossbow. Now it was worse.

One morning, as they moved from their position where they spent the night in restless sleep, Mal didn't realize that he had left behind a couple of clips of ammo. That wasn't just a costly mistake; it could be a deadly one. By the time he noticed, it was the next night.

Nobody got angry. Nobody had the energy for anger. Nobody went back, either. Jesus Christ himself could have been back where the clips were left. He and the ammo were just going to have to stay there.

Their movement was forward. The concept of *going back* just didn't exist. There was no *back*.

The daily ritual became just that -- a ritual, like an ancient Greek Dirge.

Wake up.

Piss -- if you can.

Drink water.

Eat -- whatever.

Start walking.

Mid-day.

Stop -- rest.

Eat.

Drink.

Piss.

Walk.

Gather food -- as you go.

Getting dark.

Eat.

Piss.
Drink.
Sleep.
Next day -- repeat.

Repeat...

Repeat...

Chapter 16

STEVE'S HAND WAS REALLY BAD. The puss that had begun oozing from the unhealed wound had taken on a very distinct green coloring, and a strange smell permeated the area.

Eddy's hand had healed into a claw at the end of his wrist, but it was beyond infection due to the cauterization of the wound by the red-hot bullet and powder burns. But not Steve's.

Eddy and Mal were changing the bandage and Mal gave Eddy a sudden glance. Eddy shook his head slightly, which meant, *Not now. Later.*

Eddy pulled some energy up, from where he had no idea, and tried joking. He knew Steve was in trouble. But, so did Steve.

"Well, Steve," he began. "Looks like you're going to have some hefty scarring. Used right, Linda might get to like the washboard effect as you run your hand over her. Little extra stimulation."

Steve looked up at Eddy. With a very weak attempt at a smile, he said, "Don't bullshit a bullshitter. I'm in a bad way and I know it. Mal, you don't have to hide it from me, either. I know what you noticed and I saw your little head signal. Give me a break! It's *my* hand. I've been smelling the flesh rotting for the last two days.

"What was I supposed to do? Cry?

"When it falls off, I'll send it C.O.D. to Nguyên, thanking him for the vacation. Better yet, to my congressman... I know! President Johnson! The Commander in Chief! The guy who sent me here!

"Do you guys realize," Steve continued trying to ease the situation, "when I was going to be drafted I wasn't old enough to either vote for, or against, the asshole in Washington who came up with this *Police Action?* Or, even toast the country my life was being sacrificed to defend?

"Something's really wrong with that whole idea, man. Something's really wrong!

"Thanks for being there for me. I really am glad I was teamed up with you two."

With that last surge of energy, Steve's eyes rolled back then shut. His body went limp. Eddy grabbed his head to keep it from crashing onto the ground.

"*Amicus usque ad aras.* A friend to the last extremity," whispered Eddy.

Mal placed his index and middle fingers under the side of his jaw on his neck feeling for a pulse. He relaxed and pulled his hand away.

"He's still alive. Pulse is weak, but regular. We gotta do somethin', Eddy. And, we gotta do it now. I can last, and I know you can, but Steve won't make it. I'm going to try to whip up a poultice my sainted grandmother taught me when she got rid of a corn on my big toe. Southern recipes are the best. All I need is some tree leaves, a vine, and some tree sap. It can't hurt him and it may at least slow the infection down. He might end up losing the hand, but not his life if I can help it."

"I'm open to anything," replied Eddy, with the same caring frustration. "Go for it. Can I help?"

"Naw. Just take me a second."

Eddy continued, "Look. It's late in the day and I know we are both tired. So, let's stay right here tonight. In the morning, we can make a carrier out of our shirts, pants, and some bamboo."

"OK," answered Mal. "Since you are the senior rank around here, I *have to* do what you say. But remember, my idea was to throw a party and invite some girls."

Eddy gave him a smile and a knowing nod of the head, thanking him for being there too.

"Say, Eddy?" continued Mal changing the subject while he gathered the ingredients and started mixing the poultice. "You never did tell me how you ended up in this hell hole -- you being a college boy and all."

"I'm not really a college boy," Eddy began. "Oh, I did go to college, but I didn't finish. *We all control our own destiny,* or so the saying goes.

"But that's mostly bullshit," Eddy started to explain to Mal, but mostly to himself. "I'd like to know one thing I've controlled. Sure, I've made decisions and acted on those, but I didn't have a choice. Did I?"

He began his verbal self-examination of his life leading up to this point. "OK! OK! I know. We all have choices. Contemplating *death* as the only alternate, especially when you have others to consider, is not really much of a choice. Man does have a natural instinct to survive.

"But, what am I going to do now? Steve is going to die unless I get us to some help. You are both looking to me. I'm the officer. I'm the oldest, too. Admittedly that's only twenty-three, but still the oldest. You're both a couple of kids. You should be at home, playing with your women, drinking with your buddies, going to school, working, fixing a car, fishing, loving, learning about life slowly. Instead, look what you're doing. Caught in this godforsaken jungle, fighting for your lives, and Steve's losing the battle. Maybe we're all losing the battle. I don't know.

"I just don't know!

"I ain't no kid," broke in Mal. "I'm almost as old as you."

"Shit! You two are kids. Not that I'm an Old Sage of the Forest. As I said, I'm only twenty-three, myself! Twenty-three! I should be doing all those things, as well. Who picked me? Why am I the *Keeper of the Flame?*"

He continued the self-examination process while explaining to Mal. "I know. I know. Nobody put a gun in my back and made me join the Army. Like you two, I volunteered. I'm the one who agreed to go to the academy to become an officer. When they told me my test scores were extremely high, vanity, I guess, took over. *Why not?* I thought. *I can lead.* Some leader. I'm getting us all killed."

"You are doing the best you can, Eddy. You're doing better than most officers I've ever know."

"Thanks, but I don't feel it.

"After OCS I went and volunteered for Ranger/Airborne. Finished at the top of my class and was offered Special Forces, becoming part of the only class to be trained out of the United States. Panama is almost as bad a country as this shit-hole.

"After graduation from that self-indulged torture, we were informed that not only were we the only class trained on foreign soil, but our training itself had been different from the normal given to the Special Forces. We had been handpicked. We were now part of a select group. Our very existence was classified. We were the first of a sub-classification in the Special Forces called *Black Ops*.

"As you know, we work in smaller groups. And could, in fact would, be used as assassins and any other dirty job they could think up that no one else would do."

Eddy began analyzing the series of events that led up to his present status.

"Considering the effort I put into staying out of the firing line, I sure ended up in it. Didn't I?

"I joined the Army to give myself a choice of jobs, instead of letting myself be drafted and having to do whatever someone else wanted me to. When accepting the candidacy to the Officer's Academy, I selected Artillery, figuring the big guns were in the back, miles away from the fighting. I had a high aptitude for math, which qualified me. This was a kick, as I had never done especially well in math in high school. I never did especially well in any subject, other than music, theatre, or sports, probably because I didn't give a damn about any of the other stuff. No one in my family was highly educated, so there was no real motivation for achievement in the other areas. Not that anyone talked education down. It's just that the subject never came up."

"I understand," stated Mal. "As I said, there was no family motivation for me to attend college. Most of my family can't even spell *college*."

"I attended a high school," continued Eddy, "in middle-class Southern California, where going on to college was an accepted fact, like becoming a senior after finishing your junior year. Everyone just did it.

"So, I did it too. But, without the education motivation, I joined a fraternity, the Omega Sigma Rho, and partied my way from eighteen units down to three by the end of the second week of each semester.

"'GREETINGS FROM THE PRESIDENT OF THE UNITED STATES,' the infamous letter began."

"Yea. I got one of them too. You'd think the head of the most powerful country in the world would have more to do with his time than writing letters to ruin the lives of a bunch of hopelessly romantic alcoholics."

"Well, remember back then there was no Draft Lottery. You got drafted if you were eighteen years of age, a male of sound physical condition (which meant you were breathing. Not much else was required.), not in college full time, and not married. Later they changed that rule to *married without a child*. A big baby boom happened when that stipulation came out."

"Welcome to my world," stated Mal.

"Well, guess what this idiot did? I joined as soon as I got my Preliminary Draft Notice.

"I took the written tests and ranked very high, as I said. How would I have known? No one had ever told me. Sure, the school counselors always told me that I *could do better* because I had such *potential*. But, nobody ever really explained it to me. They said that to everybody. Even the drooling idiots who couldn't write a sentence let alone a thesis. What made me special?

"Sergeant Miley. I'll never forget him. There was a man who had his shit together.

"I'll remember the first time I saw him for the rest of my life. Walking into the recruiting office in Pasadena and telling him I had received my Draft Notice but I wanted to have a choice as to how I spent my time, I sat down as he smiled and told me that this happened sometimes. He could take care of it. He asked if I could go to the Enlistment Headquarters in Los Angeles the next day and take the required battery of tests.

"It wasn't like I was worried about attending classes, or attending anything else for that matter. My social calendar was open, so I said, 'Sure'.

"He told me to come back to his office when I finished the test. It would take half of the day but I should come back in the afternoon.

"I went and took the test then drove back to the recruiting office. When I walked in, Miley was sitting at his desk reading my test results. They had gotten there before me. I didn't know how he managed that, but none-the-less there he was. Sitting, reading my results with this big shit-eating grin on his face.

"'It's what I expected', he said.

"'So, how'd I do?' I asked.

"'What would you like to do in the Army?' he inquired, not answering my question.

"'I don't know,' I responded. 'What did I score highest in?'

"'Everything.'

"'What do you mean, 'Everything'?'

"'With these scores, you *know* what the word *everything* means. Don't act dumb with me. It won't work. I'm here to help you. So, let's stop playing games and get down to it. I thought you said you didn't do especially well in high school?'

"'I didn't,' I responded amazed at his reaction and tone.

"'Well, you did on this test. What would you like to do?'

"'Where did I score the very best?'

"'Leadership and Mechanical Skills. You can't go to the academy to be an officer because you haven't finished college. So, how about something in the Mechanical Skills department?'

"He then handed me a list of MOSs (Military Occupation Specialties, or jobs in civilian lingo) and told me to pick one. Looking it over, I saw *Multiple Engine Airplane Repair*.

"'What's this Airplane Repair?' I asked. 'Since when does the Army have airplanes?'

"'Don't forget, the Air Force used to be the Army Air Corps. This is a small holdover. We have spotter-planes, helicopters, etc. It's a good field.'

"'OK,' I decided. 'Put me in. It'll give me a trade to use when I get out.' And, quietly I thought to myself, *'You can't get further behind the front lines than that. It's perfect! Most multi-engine airplanes are back with the generals.'*

"After being inducted, as you remember, the first three days of basic training at Fort Polk, Louisiana, were spent taking those same tests all over again, evidently with the same results.

"Less than a week after finishing the tests, the Commanding Officer of the Training Company ordered me to his office.

"'At ease, Private,' he began after returning my salute. 'Take a seat.'

"I sat."

"I can see where this is going," said Mal.

"'Your test scores are remarkable,' said the Captain. 'We were told to watch for you. Given any thought to attending the Officer's Candidate School?'

"'I don't have a College Degree, sir.'

"'That was *before* you got in. Now that you're in, the Army's requirements are not as stringent. You have enough college units to qualify. You would still have to undergo more tests, a very thorough physical, and appear before a Board who will bombard you with questions. These last are called the *Orals,* and that Board will have the final decision as to your acceptance. It's rough, but it's worth a try.'

"'Can I think about it, sir?'

"'An officer does his thinking on his feet, soldier. Men's lives depend on his decisions and he *never* has time to *think about it*!

"'Understood, sir. Yes, I would like to go.'

"'Let's change that to, 'You would like to *try*.'

"'Yes, sir!'

"I later reflected on the fact that, in my Basic Training Company I was the only private *not* heading for Airborne/Ranger, Special Forces, Warrant Officer Flight, or OCS.

"Basic was a treat, as you remember. I had a particularly grizzly DI (Drill Instructor) who brought to a new level of non-comprehension the English language. I swear, Mal, before a guy can graduate from Smokey Bear School, (so designated by the type of hat they wore) they have to take a class on the destruction of the language. I can't remember him ever finishing a sentence, or a word for that matter. 'Pri..., mo yo ass ova hr! Tin hut! Teeze!' It took me two weeks to decipher the language. '*Private, move your ass over here. Attention! At ease!*' What cracked me up the most was the lack of attempt in pronouncing someone's name. Soldiers with Polish last names were always 'Alphabet 1, or Alphabet 2,' instead of Szalkowski, or Ramikowski.

"Eventually I got to understand DI-speak and finished basic. Then on to AIT (Advanced Individual Training) at Fort Sill, Oklahoma before beginning OCS. I had chosen Artillery, because I was required to pick from a combat arms. Infantry was out of the question. Remember my desire to stay away from the front? Signal and Armored just didn't appeal to me. My dad had been Air-defense Artillery, so I chose Artillery. I couldn't think of anything further back from the front. I didn't know until AIT that the first job of an Artillery Second Lieutenant is *Forward Observer. So much for staying out of the heat.*

"After completing OCS and getting my Commission, I was home on leave and went back to the Recruiting Office to show Sergeant Miley the Frankenstein's Monster he had created. As I walked in, in full dress uniform, all the other Non-Coms jumped to attention, except Miley. He just looked up and started to laugh his head off.

"The Son-of-a-bitch had planned the whole thing from the beginning."

"What?" yelled Mal.

"That's when I learned that the *Sergeants run the Army.*

"The *real* irony occurred when I completed Black Ops training in Panama. My brother and I were sole surviving sons. My brother, who was older as I said, had been drafted. He got married to avoid the draft, but when they changed the rules including married men who didn't have children, he drew the line in the sand. He wasn't going to rush into having a child, so he got drafted.

"He hated the Army and everything about it. As I was going to the various schools, he received orders to go to Korea. His letters home expressed how much he feared for his life and how horrible it was to be in a combat situation. He wanted to get home to his wife and a normal life. The letters got increasingly horrific.

"As long as one sibling in a *sole surviving* situation was in a short-tour area, the other could not receive orders to a like assignment.

"I, in my caring stupidity, to create a situation causing him to be able to come home and be with his wife in safety, volunteered for this shit-hole. Well, as you can imagine, my MOS was just a little higher on the food chain than his, so my orders were cut and he was brought home."

"How is that ironic?" asked Mal.

"After he was home and I was in country, I found out that the asshole (And I say that lovingly. I really do love my brother.) was a battalion clerk. He spent his time in Korea in an air-conditioned office typing daily reports and getting the Colonel coffee.

"Yea. He was really suffering. I could have had a great assignment in Germany or stateside, but no. Murphy's Law shit in my direction. That's how we find ourselves in this particular situation.

"If I hadn't been here, you would have had another commander who wouldn't have made the stupid mistake I did. Right now, you and Steve would be back at Base Camp, going to the NCO club, drinking beers, playing poker and not spending every waking and sleeping moment staying away from death's door."

"You don't know that," interjected Mal. "You did what ya thought was right. Steve and I don't hold it against you. We would probably have done the same. And who the hell knows who our commander would have been. He could have been a real asshole."

"Well, anyway, as you can see I never had a choice, any more than I do right now. We have to get out of this mess."

"We will, Eddy," said Mal. "We will. And you will be the one to do it. I know it."

"Well, I'm going to go try to find some food. That stuff you're making smells like shit, and that's saying something considering that none of us have had a decent bath in longer than I can think."

"Smells like shit, or is shit," said Mal. "If it can help Steve, who cares?"

Eddy walked into the jungle praying that he would find something they could call food. All he came up with was some rotting fruit which had fallen on the jungle floor, some grubs from under an old log, and one eighteen inch snake about the diameter of his thumb.

So far beyond exhaustion the word itself had no meaning, Eddy went back to Mal and Steve. Mal didn't say anything about the little he brought back. He understood.

Eddy *didn't* understand.

After they dined al fresco, they shut their eyes and passed out -- for the last time in the jungle.

Chapter 17

EDDY'S BODY MIGHT HAVE BEEN out, but his mind kept going. The field soldier in Viet Nam never enjoyed a restful sleep. How could he? If he wasn't having nightmares, his mind was always conscious of the little noises that went on around him, half ready to spring into action if the need arose.

His mind went back and forth, from nightmare to listening. In remembering back, he related the effect to the way a cat sleeps. It can be out, but the ears constantly move and one eye opens and shuts if anything goes on around it.

Eddy's ears didn't move, but his mind sure did. He dreamed intermittently. They were vague, unclear images he couldn't lock onto. He remembered Sergeant Miley, Mal, Steve, Miley again, Nguyên, his girlfriend Marge, Steve's wife Linda, and Miley again...

What's with thinking of Miley so much?

OK. The guy was a good recruiter and did his job better than anyone. So what? That doesn't make him the embodiment of the *Second Coming,* or the *Angel of Mercy.* Does it?

A thought passed in an instant. Eddy wished that Miley were here. He could use council from a more experienced soldier.

But, this was Nam. It was a young man's war. The average age of a soldier in the field during the Second World War was thirty-one. Korea, twenty-seven. Even the Civil War, with all the children involved (drummer boys, flag carriers, etc.) statistically showed the average age to be twenty-three. Of course, statistics were nowhere near accurate then. Boys lied to go fight, and there was no way to check. Historians believe the average age to be more like sixteen or seventeen.

That was tragic. At sixteen, who has experienced enough life to put it on the line ready to be snuffed out? Of course, the Civil War itself was tragic.

There is no such thing as a good war, Eddy thought in his dreams. *Some are necessary, but none are good.*

Viet Nam era statistics were quite accurate. Lying was a lot harder to do. The average age of the American soldier in Viet Nam was twenty-two years, six months. Everything was on computer. The Department of the Army had computers that took up entire floors of buildings, keeping statistics on punch cards or tape that contained every fact possible. If a security clearance was required for your MOS they even interviewed your elementary school teachers and the interview was included in deciding whether or not you got the clearance. One of Eddy's fellow candidates at OCS couldn't receive his commission due to a holdup on his security clearance. There was something about a report from his junior high school years that was a red flag. *Really? Junior High School?* What the hell could a kid at the ripe old age of twelve do to cause a danger to the country? He eventually received his commission, but it took an extra year.

What a joke. Eddy's mind switched back to the present, sitting in the rain in Southern California. The year Two Thousand had passed a long time ago. Compared to the computers and statistics they keep today, those were like stone carvings. A computer that can sit on your lap or in your hand does more than those that took up entire floors. Plus the Internet actually creates a world computer. Everyone's tied together.

Back in Nam, a guy would have to be born and raised in the back woods of the Appalachians to escape the all-knowing statistical eye of the government. Now-a-days, even that wouldn't be enough.

Through the Sixties you didn't have to get a social security number until you were eighteen, or got a job that required one. Now, you're given a number at birth. Parents can't even declare a deduction on their tax return for dependent children without their social security number.

Of course, if there had been the rapid access to information back during Nam that there is now, Eddy considered, *the war probably would have never happened. The government couldn't have fooled the public the way they did. Or maybe, then again, they could have. People are pretty gullible. They want to believe the lie, rather than the truth. It's easier.*

Eddy's mind raced back to his last night in the jungle. This was no lie. It happened. All he had to do was look at his hand, and...

He remembered lying there. Knowing the desperate condition of his entire group, and running out of options, Eddy turned to someone of which he had lost faith. He had nowhere else to go -- no one else to turn to. There is an old saying: *There's no such thing as an atheist in a foxhole.* This isn't just a saying. It's a fact. When life has abandoned you, there is only one way to turn.

"God," he began. "I don't know if You're up there or not. I don't know if You can hear me or even want to listen, but I'm not asking for myself. I'm asking for Steve and Mal. These guys are the best. If you are God, then you already know that. Help them. Save them.

"If that means you take me, so be it. I gladly give myself for them. Please, help them. In case Your listening, thanks in advance."

He then let his mind relax and fell asleep.

He hadn't been out long when he began hearing voices that were softly murmuring. The voices weren't speaking to him, but to each other. There was more than one person around him. Was it a dream? Or was it the twilight listening that his mind and senses did, unsuccessfully attempting to keep him aware of what was going on around him?

The biggest problem was that exhaustion had taken its toll. None of them, not Mal, Steve, or Eddy, cared if they drew another breath. Death would be a welcomed rest. Physically and mentally pushed beyond any remotely conceivable limits of tolerance, they now existed in the realm of living fiction. That area where the protected, spoiled, and delusional mind of the people living back in *The World*, believed only existed in the Imagination of fiction writers.

These things didn't really happen.

Right!!!!!

Eddy, trying to determine whether it was dream or reality, brought himself slowly awake without moving a muscle to keep from giving away his regained awareness to anyone who might be around in case it was reality.

The voices were still there.

Reality!!!

There were people around the three of them. Stretching out his senses without opening his eyes, he could feel their presence. He estimated about a half dozen, and they were not Americans.

There was something familiar in their language. Not Vietnamese, but a lot like something he'd heard before.

He *felt* a presence very close to him. Preparing his body to spring into action, unconsciously his body pumped what little adrenalin was left into every vein and muscle in his body.

Slowly opening one eye a crack, he gave it time to focus.

His entire body relaxed.

His mind relaxed.

His thoughts relaxed.

He started weeping. With his second breath, the weeping became uncontrollable crying. His emotions couldn't have been stronger if Jesus Christ himself was standing there.

It was over.

He reached up, putting his arms around the neck of the little brown Montagnard whose face was not six inches from his, and held on, crying as no one has ever done before.

The little brown men in the loin cloths, on a hunting trip to provide food for their village, had come upon the three as they slept. American's were not the enemy of the little people, so aid was immediately given.

The Montagnards took the three to their village. Steve was unconscious and had to be carried in a litter made by the little men.

They were saved and the *healing* process could begin.

Chapter 18

THE MONTAGNARDS ARE A PRIMITIVE people, as I said before, and their life is very simple. They live off the rice they grow, plus chickens, pigs, and whatever the men can hunt. Being very adept with their bamboo crossbows, they can bring down a bird in flight.

They are a loving people with a great sense of humor. Eddy found that particularly fascinating. What did they have to be happy about?

The entire Montagnard population of the world lived in a country where, not only were they the extreme minority, they were hated by the Vietnamese. He remembered again the degradation these wonderful people succumbed to on a daily basis. And yet, the Montagnards did not hate the Vietnamese. They forgave them.

The little brown men knew nothing of Christianity except what a rare Catholic or Mormon missionary would expound passing from village to village over the years.

Throughout the history of Viet Nam, missionaries have played an integral part in the attempted westernization of the culture. Their motivation was rarely a religious one. Economic concessions were the bargaining chips used between the old Vietnamese emperors and the French monarchy. The French missionaries, more often than not, negotiated these stakes.

The Montagnards never had anything worth negotiating for, so they were usually left alone. When missionaries did show up, they didn't stay long. Eddy wondered if it were possibly because the Montagnards didn't even have a word in their language for *guilt*. And, since guilt is the main driving force behind almost all religious zealots, how could they get across any other ideas.

You have to feel guilty about the way you've lived for the last countless centuries. Your way is wrong. But, that's OK, because our way is right, and you can change to our way. Stop being the happy, loving, caring people you are, living the true meaning of forgiveness of which few Missionaries ever conceptually grasped, and become like us: bitter, mean, judgmental, pompous, unhappy, unloving, socially and sexually perverted hypocrites.

Missionaries destroyed the Hawaiian people. They virtually wiped out an entire culture. In gratitude to the Hawaiians for letting them do that, they stole all of their islands. You can't blame it on the whalers. They liked the Hawaiians the way they were. Of course, they brought disease to the islands never known before, but they didn't try to change the culture or steal the land.

That *wonderful* accomplishment was solely the missionary's. There were some good missionaries, exceptions to every rule. But sadly, they were the extreme exceptions. Not enough to count, historically.

Eddy, Mal, and Steve were glad the missionaries hadn't succeeded with the Montagnards, yet. They knew that they were still trying periodically and eventually would win. Modern technology presents a strong argument when a people are shown something they think is magic or supernatural.

Eddy remembered one time while the three were recuperating, slowly regaining their strength, a missionary showed up at their village.

Eddy didn't know what religion he supposedly represented, but it really didn't matter. Since his first firefight, he had been turned off of any god that would allow the events he witnessed for over a year to continue. Were it not for his prayer being answered by their rescue, he would have continued this thought process. But, as each day passed he realized more and more that this *Permission for Horror* had been going on since the beginning of history.

Most of the missionaries pulled the same shit, irrespective of their religion. So as far as Eddy was concerned that made all organized religions the same.

This particular missionary presented a Polaroid camera to the Montagnards. They had never seen one before and to them it was just a strange shaped black box.

The missionary had the village chief, his wife, son, and daughter stand together as he took their picture.

Slowly the photograph developed, revealing itself. The Chief and the entire village were absolutely astounded, very big *magic*.

A lot of...

Eddy fully understood, later, why Gene Roddenberry, the creator of *Star Trek,* came up with the idea of the *Prime Directive:* You can't do anything that would affect the development of a culture. It must be allowed to develop on its own.

Missionaries didn't understand that concept. This guy used fear as his primary motivation. The pleasant surprise of the people changed instantly to terror as the missionary, who up until then had been all happy and smiling, became very serious and mean.

He held up the picture above all the men, women, and children, who had stopped laughing and joking due to this maniac, who possessed a great power, was shouting at them. They were frozen in place not understanding his anger.

The missionary announced that the box had captured the chief and his family's souls, the very essence that made them above the lizard or snake. He further announced that if the chief and his whole village didn't follow his teachings (He said Christ's, but Eddy knew this guy had stopped teaching Jesus' ideals a long time ago.) he would tear the picture and destroy their souls. They would become like mindless pigs, eating the dirt on the ground.

The chief and his son stood there frozen. His wife and daughter started to cry uncontrollably. Then the whole village started weeping and pleading with the missionary not to do this. They loved their chief and didn't want to see him destroyed.

In response to their pleadings, the missionary quickly took as many pictures of as many of the villagers as he could. As these developed, he held them all up and announced he now had all of their souls.

Eddy noticed that during this whole episode the missionary's assistant, a fat slob who had obviously never spent a second of his life doing something good for others, or going without a meal, had worked his way around to one particular older man standing in the back of the villagers gathered around the missionary.

Eddy observed this whole event from a hut, unseen by the missionary or his assistant. He had a gut feeling when they first showed up that the existence of the three should not be revealed.

Now, Eddy was glad he made the choice to hide.

With a nod from the assistant, and an acknowledging nod from the missionary, he lowered the pictures. Quiet came over the villagers as they hoped the missionary had acquiesced to their pleadings.

No such luck!!

The missionary, pretending to bow his head in prayer, was scanning the photos for the picture of the old man. Finding it, he suddenly snapped out of his prayer and held it up.

Silence fell over the village, as though even the chickens were waiting to see what this *magic man* or *god* would do.

The missionary shouted, "To prove that God will take your worthless heathen souls, one man will be separated from his and it will disappear into oblivion being thrown into the fiery pits of Hell to suffer *eternal torment*."

The chief, straight, strong, and dry-eyed during this whole ritual, stepped up to the missionary. He said, "Let it be me. Do not hurt one of my people. I am their chief. Take *my* soul."

Eddy knew that neither the chief nor his people were really sure what a soul was, but it sounded pretty important. He also knew they didn't know what Hell was, but it too sounded really bad, a place to avoid. The Montagnards believed in an *after-life*, but *life's essence* was held in the hearts of the family. They worshipped life. All life: Plant, Animal, the Earth, Man. When a person's body died, he lived on as a part of his children, then grandchildren, etc. It was a lot like the reason soldiers share their lives with one another, to live forever.

Eddy admired this chief. He was a very brave man who truly put his people before himself. Even a Medal of Honor recipient, who gives his life to protect the lives of his fellow soldiers, only worries about death. Death is one thing. To lose your soul, or *life's essence*, to this unknown but obviously very bad oblivion took a hell of a lot more courage and sacrifice.

The missionary pushed the chief away to the total shock of the village. "You haven't led your people to Christ all these years. You are not worthy to be the example."

This *Christ* fellow, they didn't know either, but he must be pretty important too. He was probably this *man-who-keeps-yelling's* chief. Most likely he lived in the big city they could see from the treetops up on the mountains.

Montagnards didn't go to the cities except on very rare occasions when a few of the elders would undergo the journey to trade. They were never allowed in the city, however. They were met outside where the trading took place. This Christ fellow must live with the Vietnamese. The Montagnards believed, as Eddy found out later, that that was why the Vietnamese treated them the way they did. This fellow must have taken the souls of the Vietnamese.

They didn't want to become like them.

The missionary slowly and dramatically lowered the picture. Then taking it in between his fingers he tore the old man's picture in half.

At that same instant the old man in the back screamed in pain and collapsed to the ground.

After quickly hiding the hypodermic syringe used to knockout his victim, the assistant bent down pretending to try to lend aid to this poor heathen. He was injected with just enough to knock him out. The ploy was the missionary's prayers would bring him back from the pit of Hell.

The whole time the missionary was standing there, praying to God that he forgive this heathen and rescue him from His wrath. The missionary lowered his head and hands from being outstretched toward the heavens and said, "Because of my intervention, God will give this worthless man another chance. And, he will forgive you. But you must follow me. Do what I say!"

Eddy couldn't believe it. From that instant, this son-of-slime had an entire village of slaves.

"Not while I'm here!!" Eddy declared aloud.

As the villagers gathered closer around the missionary, in total supplication, the jackass stood there smiling, reveling in his victory. So full of self-importance, neither he nor his assistant noticed the rather large Montagnard coming out of one of the huts. They also didn't notice him walk around to a position right behind the assistant. In fact, the assistant didn't even notice until the very last instant when he felt a sharp pain in the side of his neck, this same tall Montagnard reach into his pocket and remove the extra syringe he had. Then bouncing the point against a rock, making it nice and dull causing a lot of pain going in, this tall one put his hand over the assistant's mouth, to keep him from yelling, then slammed it into his neck.

One out of the way, thought Eddy, as he stood there watching this conceited asshole with his arms out gathering in his flock. *This guy is a real shepherd sent here to protect the lambs. Really? Well, he picked the wrong Montagnard village to turn into sheep. There's a wolf in the herd and this wolf likes the sheep.*

The missionary was so into himself, he still didn't notice Eddy, even as he walked directly to the platform being used. He stood there for what seemed like a long time, waiting for the jerk to see him. Finally giving up, he walked around to the back where the steps were and walked up, standing right next to the arrogant ass.

Finally noticing that someone was on his platform out of his peripheral vision he waved his hand behind him, indicating that the person get off the platform. He still hadn't seen Eddy for what he was.

The missionary snapped out of his reverie. He started noticing the villagers had stopped fawning over him. They were just standing there, staring. He further noticed they weren't staring at him. He wondered for a moment what had happened that could have caused their attention to change. Maybe it was the Montagnard on the platform. He quickly held up the pictures in both hands prepared to tear them all.

Snap! The pictures were ripped out of his hands. Eddy tapped on his shoulder. He turned, ready to verbally blast whoever was there...

"SURPRISE!!!!!"

Eddy backhanded him so hard he flew off the platform. Landing in the dirt, he struggled to get up. But Eddy was on him like stink on shit.

He grabbed him by his cheap jacket lapel and pulled him to his feet. Holding him close, he noticed a strong smell. No, it wasn't the bourbon on his breath. Eddy had expected that. It was a lot worse. Then it hit him. Eddy had scared this guy so badly that he had shit in his pants. Literally.

"Why don't you take my picture and send *my* soul to Hell, you hypocritical du miami? Then we'll see who succumbs to your bullshit."

"Who are you?" asked the missionary. He was speaking English for the first time since he had arrived.

"Your worst nightmare! An American who loves these people and resents your trying to screw-up their lives, a guy who you and your kind can't scare. Your mumbo jumbo won't work here. Leave! Now! And don't come back to this village, you or any of your kind. And take that fat piece of shit with you."

"You're keeping these people from salvation. Are you an agent of the Anti-Christ?"

"Don't even try to pull that shit on me, asshole! These people know more about the true meaning of *LOVE* than you ever have. The way I see it, I'm not keeping them from salvation. I'm saving them from you, and you're further from salvation's door than the last Vietnamese that I killed. Want to join him? Glad to help there. Now you've been warned. I really hate repeating myself." Eddy reached over to one of the Montagnards standing near him in the crowd who happened to have a machete in his loincloth. He grabbed the machete and passed it under this missionary's shirt buttons, blade side up. The buttons flew and his pale chest lay exposed.

Emitting a stifled cry, the missionary's eyes got bigger than Eddy thought possible. He then turned the blade over and placed it right over his soft belly.

"They say that the intestine is actually quite long. Shall we measure?" Eddy acted like he was going to cut this guy wide open. He was pissed.

A hand gently came before Eddy's eyes and grabbed the machete. He followed the arm back and was looking into the eyes of the chief, who was shaking his head. The chief's other hand was placed gently on Eddy's shoulder like a father to a son.

The chief said, "No. This is not the way. He will go now. Besides, he stinks."

Eddy stared at the chief for a good five-count. Then, releasing his grip on the machete, he broke into laughter.

"Get out of here," he told the missionary, turning him around and pushing him away. "And change your pants. You smell like shit."

"You scared me. I had an accident."

"It may have been an accident for you, but remember, what I did wasn't an accident. I did it on purpose. Next time, the Chief may not be around.

"And remember, Man of God. *Qui facit per alium facit per se.* He who does through another does it through himself."

The missionary gathered up his assistant and left the village to the laughs and jeers of the Montagnards. They had learned something that day, Eddy hoped.

Eddy had learned something too. The Montagnards, after centuries of degradation, had learned to forgive anything. Eddy wondered if he would ever be able to live up to the standards of these *Primitive Barbarians* who truly knew *forgiveness.*

Chapter **19**

THE HEALING WAS DONE. WHEN considering the stuff the old woman, who was placed in charge of making them well, gave them to drink, the *cure* was in many ways worse than the disease. In gratitude for keeping the villager's souls from being thrown into Hell the chief personally saw to their care. He had his wife tend to Eddy. As he started to get his strength back, the chief's daughter took over. He was still sufficiently out of it not to care, a totally different experience from his first visit to the Army hospital when he came down with malaria.

As with all experiences even the worse has its moments of enjoyment. Eddy remembered sitting at the bar in the Officer's Club at Cam Ranh Bay after the quinine became more powerful than the malaria, drinking with the other hapless individuals who were at that particular location for one specific purpose: to try to make some sense of the whole thing while their wounds healed or their bodies recovered from one or another of the more common diseases which proliferated the country.

A person standing back and viewing the sight would have shaken their heads at the sanity of these men. A malaria patient, sitting next to a contagious hepatitis patient, sitting next to a soldier with hundreds of little threads sticking up from his multiple stitching, sitting next to one whose face was half burned away, and all drinking and laughing together, each finding a moment to be happy about, each talking about how *short* they were (the time they had left before rotating home), or how they'd gotten wounded. First order of business was to watch the TV show *Combat* being broadcast over the Armed Forces Television Network, so they could see how a war was supposed to be fought. That particular show brought more laughter than *I Love Lucy*.

As the evening wore on and the drinking became more intense, singing started. This ear-shattering event was only surpassed by the joke telling. As nurses frequented the bar after completing their shifts, the jokes started out very politely. That is until the nurse who was the duty nurse for the officer's section came over and offered a particularly rude story about a man in a bar with a dog that spoke. This, essentially, gave them permission to pull out all the stops. The jokes got worse and worse to everyone's enjoyment. The singing got louder and the jokes got raunchier. The head nurse finally excused herself under the pretense of having an early shift the next day, but the rest continued the party.

The top-ranking individual, a full-bird Colonel who had been hit by shrapnel in a rocket attack on his headquarters, came up with a thought that seemed to everyone to be the best idea of the war. They were all going to go down to the area where the nurse's quarters were and sing to their special *angel*, who had cared for them and brought so much delight to the evening's festivities. Just because the nurse's quarters were *off limits* should be of no hindrance.

It was a stupid rule anyway.

By about two in the morning they had all acquired enough liquid courage to begin the concert. The quarters were in an area a little ways from the bar so they began their walk. As the walk progressed they eventually fell into step with one another. This rhythm led to the eventuality of more songs that were rendered at the top of their voices.

As with most military formation singing it starts with one person, usually a sergeant, calling out a chant to the rhythm of the footsteps. This is responded to by everyone in the formation repeating or answering the call. On this occasion there was no sergeant as it was a group of drunken officers, so the Colonel assumed his rightful place as the leader.

It went something like this:

Colonel -- "I don't know, but I've been told."
Drunks -- "I don't know, but I've been told."
Colonel -- "Eskimo pussy is mighty cold."
Drunks -- "Eskimo pussy is mighty cold."
Colonel -- "I might be wrong, might be right."
Drunks -- "I might be wrong, might be right."
Colonel -- "But, Jody's fuckin' my girl tonight."
Drunks -- "But, Jody's fuckin' my girl tonight."
Colonel -- "Sound off!"
Drunks -- "One, Two."
Colonel -- "Sound off!"
Drunks -- "Three, Four."
Colonel -- "Sound off!"
Drunks -- "One, Two, Three, Four. One, Two, -- Three Four!"
This went on for a while to the delight of everyone.
Well, almost everyone.

As they came upon the area separating the hospital from the nurse's and doctor's quarters they stopped at a large sign which made it very clear that the area was off limits to all but hospital personnel. Clear, that is, to all those that care about such trivialities. This group didn't care about anything except the *mission* they had undertaken. The *objective* was in sight and they were not about to let some stupid sign keep them from their awaited *goal*.

As they marched past the sign singing loudly, a second lieutenant came running out of the office next to where the sign was stuck in the sand yelling that they had to stop. He was the duty officer and this area was off limits.

Eddy stepped forward to the front of the staggering group and asked the poor guy where he had come up with the idea that the area was off limits.

"It's right there on that sign," stated the Lieutenant. "Can't you guys read? It's late and you're all too drunk and too loud. Go back to your barracks."

One of the drunks yelled, "'There's no such thing as *'Too Drunk'.*"

Eddy, trying futilely to focus, intervened and asked, "What sign?"

Taking the hint, a few of the other comrades-in-drink stepped over to the sign, pulled it out of the sand, and laid it face down on the ground.

As Eddy turned around and the group parted so the lieutenant could see the absence of the referenced piece of artwork, the officer started to yell at them and threaten things that would stop any normal person from going any further. Only these were not normal people. These were guys who had been shot at and shit on, and got hit each time.

The Colonel stepped forward and revealed himself to the lieutenant. The threats immediately stopped when the Colonel was recognized. Approaching the lieutenant, the Colonel calmly put his hand on the duty officer's shoulder and looked into his eyes.

The silence was deafening.

Finally the Colonel spoke. Quietly, and with a smile on his face that had appeared slowly keeping the lieutenant off his guard, the Colonel asked the infamous question asked by every Viet Nam veteran.

"What are you going to do, Lieutenant, send us to Viet Nam? Now, go back in your little office and continue pretending you are a big war hero. If you do, you won't get hurt, and we wouldn't want that to happen, now would we?

"Go in, and leave these real hero's alone."

The lieutenant said, "But, sir? I'm going to have to report this. I'll have to enter it in my log."

"Lieutenant," commanded the Colonel with as much authority as his multiple scotches would allow. "You are not going to report anything. You are not going to enter anything. You are going to go into your little office, shut the door, play with your Teddy, and shut up!!! Got it, Lieutenant?!!"

"Yes, sir," answered the brown-bar, wishing he had picked some other branch to get his commission in besides the Medical Corps. He had had nothing but trouble. Ever since his daddy, the Honorable Senator from the glorious state of North Carolina, got him into a non-combat branch, he had nothing but...

With the idiot shut up, the group continued on its endeavor.

Approaching the trailer that served as the domicile for the nurse, the drunken group gathered around and offered forth a dissonant version of *Heart of My Heart* with full harmony. Thinking, in their drunken pride, that they sounded pretty good they continued with a few more cheerful numbers.

No lights came on in the trailer. Lights came on in all the surrounding trailers, but not this one. So, they went up to the door and started to knock.

Still no answer.

She had stated very clearly that she was leaving the bar and coming straight here and going to bed.

Not wanting to accept that she had changed her mind and was not there to receive their special gift, they started banging on the side of the trailer in rhythm to the song being offered.

Finally, a light came on and voices were heard from inside.

Voices??

Only one person lived in this trailer but they distinctly heard more than one voice. And, one was definitely lower than the other.

Eventually the door opened and the nurse stepped into the threshold to see what was going on.

When she saw who was making all the noise she busted up laughing. The group, feeling very pleased with themselves for accomplishing their mission, broke into another song.

As they sang, the nurse motioned to the *someone-else* who was in the trailer to come to the door and see what was taking place.

There, standing next to the nurse and wearing one of her pink bathrobes, was the doctor who was in charge of their section.

They stopped singing and started laughing, uncontrollably. He was a major, and everyone liked him.

Eddy had always compared the memory of this guy to the character Hawkeye Pierce, in the movie and TV Series *MASH*, a great doctor, and a great human being, and a real stud with the ladies.

Hey! Everyone needs a hobby!

But in the Montagnard village, things went a bit different. Once the guys healed their physical wounds, what else was there to do? The village threw a big party.

The party, though it may not have seemed like that big of a deal in some circles, was a major event to the Montagnards. Missing was the hors d'oeuvres and various finger-foods made up of pâté and caviar, or small shrimp on those little crackers. Gone was the tinkling of crystal flutes filled with champagne, which accompanied the delicate sounds of the string quartet representing the immortal music of Mozart, Bach, and Beethoven. Nowhere could one find elegant ladies in lavish ball-gowns or gentlemen in black-tie and tails. Hell. They didn't even have rock music playing with pizza and beer.

No. Some people would not have considered it a party. But fortunately the little brown people didn't associate in those circles and when they threw a party it lasted for days.

The string quartet or rock music was replaced by two men who played on primitive flutes made from bamboo and one knocking out a steady rhythm on a large drum made from a hide stretched over a hollowed-out log. The finger foods were mostly what your fingers could pick up from the wooden bowls and plates stacked with rice, chicken, snake, and other various meats one knew better than to inquire as to their origin. Eddy always wondered what happened to that cat that used to follow him around the village.

The men danced and the women watched, then the women danced and the men watched. This was immediately followed by Eddy, Steve, and Mal dancing and everybody watched -- and laughed. Their dance didn't tell a story, it didn't make sense. It was just three drunken idiots making fools of themselves. This evidently gave the chief an idea.

He offered his daughter to Eddy as a gift. Everybody was drunk, and Eddy certainly was no exception, but the chief's daughter?!!!!!???
NO!!!!!!!!!!!!!!!!!!!!!!!!!!!!!!!!!!!!!!

Nobody is ever *that* drunk. This chick was *uglyyyyy*. Only one tooth, and that was black from years of chewing Beetle Nuts, a nut that has a mild narcotic effect when chewed and turns the teeth ebony.

So Eddy politely refused, trying to explain the differences in the cultural standards. After all, Eddy had a wife back in the world and one woman was all you were allowed. (He didn't have a wife. He had a girlfriend. But he had to make up something that would be somewhat convincing.)

The chief argued.

So, what if he did have a wife? The chief's daughter, as a second wife, could help with the daily chores and fulfill the nightly duty when the first wife was *out of sorts*. They would actually help each other.

Eddy tried to explain that it wasn't done that way in America. A man only had one wife. It was a system probably set up by the women, since they didn't like sharing.

At that, the chief asked who ran the village. Was it the women, or the men? Thinking about it, Eddy admitted that was a good question. He started to believe that he was losing the argument and was in trouble. He did *NOT* want to end up with the chief's daughter! No -- way!!!

He turned to Mal and Steve for help but they were sitting off to the side, laughing their asses off at the sight of Eddy trying to squirm out of this one. No help from them. He was on his own.

Finally the chief, himself, came to Eddy's rescue.

The chief thought the Americans were repressed and perverted. So did Eddy, but with the chief's daughter at stake agreeing with him wasn't the best idea. All Eddy could do was apologize.

The apology was easily accepted, probably due to the state of inebriation everyone was in. Plus the fact, as Eddy found out later, the chief had been trying to pawn off his daughter for years. Everyone thought she was ugly. He just thought Eddy was crazy and if he got him drunk enough...?

There is this ritual the Montagnards have for honored guests. A large earthen jar is presented. It stands about two and a half feet tall and is about fourteen inches in diameter tapering to a mouth about six inches across. The jar has rice in the bottom that has been fermenting for God knows how long. The rice is then covered with bamboo leaves all the way to the mouth.

The chief performed the ceremony this time. Water was brought ...and guess where the water came from. Right! The same place the rice did, the rice patties. That self-same place the water buffalo stand and graze -- and shit!

Anyway, the jar was filled to the brim with the water. A bamboo reed was then placed across the top of the mouth of the jar. Another smaller reed, about an inch long, was stuck through the reed across the top.

The chief proceeded to make this big production of washing and cleaning three bamboo straws that were long enough to go all the way to the bottom of the jar. And, of course, to insure that there were no foreign objects in the straws, he drew through each, protecting his guests

After the chief had put his mouth on those straws, the idea of putting their mouths on them was not the most appealing concept. But the three figured, what did they have to lose? Steve had already lost his hand.

The Montagnards spent no time on this event. Upon arriving at the village the chief, with the help of the healer (medicine man), instantly determined the progression of the infection. Steve was unconscious, but they all held him down in case he woke up, tied a strap tightly around his forearm, poured a liquid made of some concoction of jungle plants and the juice of a few crushed beetles on the hand then without hesitation down came the machete and off came the hand. More liquid was poured then a burning torch was applied cauterizing the severed wrist.

Mal looked up at Eddy after the procedure. Fortunately Steve's state of unconsciousness never changed. He stayed out for three days. "Boy," Mal stated, "will he be pissed when he wakes up. He'll have to learn to flip us off with his other hand."

Eddy appreciated Mal's attempting to lighten the mood, but a lost hand was a serious thing and the knowledge of the fact was going to be traumatic to Steve when he did wake up.

A soldier's life was certainly more than standing guard and shooting people. Vets carry burdens, big ones.

Eddy's own hand was a mangled mess -- unusable. But considering everything, they would have been dead without these great people. Who were they to even hesitate at sharing a little drink?

Little drink was the concept the little brown mountain people didn't understand. It was an insult to remove your lips from the straw until the water was drained down below the reed sticking into the jar.

The three never realized how much had to be consumed to do that simple feat, and through a straw.

They got drunk.

Then, they got sick.

Eddy remembered, from that day to this, he could never touch Sake. The stuff in the jar was like very cheap Sake, and just the thought of it would make him sick.

After living painfully through a two-day hangover, the three were taken back to an American unit the villagers had been doing some scouting for. They were medevacked back to Camp Enari outside of Pleiku then eventually made their way back to the world following a brief stay in the hospital at Cam Ranh Bay.

This time Eddy didn't visit the bar.

Back In The World

Chapter 1

AFTER ARRIVING AT McCHORD AIRBASE in Tacoma, Washington, as I said at the beginning of the story, they departed the plane and bid each other farewell.

They didn't realize that would be the last time they would ever see each other in this life.

Mal would be dead of cancer from *Agent Orange* in less than ten years. He did marry Beverley Jean. Unbeknownst to Mal, she was in love with him, too. Telling his family not to let Mal know, she kept it quiet. She didn't want to add an additional burden on to the back of someone doing a job most people would consider impossible. She had pledged an allegiance of loyalty until he came home. They had a great life together, albeit a short one. He told Eddy in a letter that he didn't regret a moment. He was a good man and a hero to the end.

Steve would become so despondent by not being able to get a decent paying job because of his lack of a hand, and not being able to be a complete husband to his wife because of the repeated whippings his penis and scrotum received at the hands of Colonel Nguyên, that he would commit suicide. He never again felt adequate for Linda, physically or emotionally. He truly loved her and felt that he was just a burden. She didn't see it that way, but he did. He couldn't conceive of putting her through a life of toil, having to take care of a handicapped, unemployed and unemployable bum, so he didn't.

One day, while she was at work, he left a note, got in the car, drove into the mountains, off a cliff, and into that land we all will travel to, but never come back from. His note left instructions for Linda to never tell anyone of his intentions. He had a life insurance policy that wouldn't pay if he took his own life. So he made it look like an accident. Linda told Eddy all of this in a phone call just before Steve was buried.

"Have you told anyone else about the letter?" Eddy asked.

"No," answered Linda. "I haven't even told my parents."

"Good," said Eddy. "Linda, listen to me. Listen to me really good. Burn the letter. The letter never existed. Steve died in a tragic auto accident and we will all miss him terribly.

"Do you understand?"

"Yes, but..."

"There is no '*but!*' There can be no '*but!*' The letter never happened. That has to be the way it is or everything Steve lived for will be lost. He loved you very much. In Nam it was all he talked about. Hold on to that love and respect his wishes. He was one of the best men I have ever known. Do this, and you will be honoring his memory."

"Ok, Eddy. I will. Thank you. You have always been a good friend and Steve loved you very much. He always spoke so highly of you. That's why I made this phone call."

"You take care, now," said Eddy. "Bye."

Still feeling somewhat responsible, Eddy couldn't even bring himself to go to his funeral. By the time Steve died, Eddy's downward spiral had attained an inescapable speed.

It was a vortex he couldn't seem to escape.

It started when he first arrived home and his girlfriend somehow couldn't meet him at the airport. He'd lived the *Dark side of the Force* and only wanted to be happy and to bring happiness. Not wanting to fight anymore in any fashion, Eddy called her at home. She wasn't there, so he called her at work.

"Hi, Marge? It's Eddy. I'm home. Didn't you get my letter telling you when I'd arrive?"

"Oh... Hi, Eddy. Uhhh, sure -- I did. It's just that my boss wouldn't let me off -- to meet the plane."

"That's OK," he answered. Feeling unbelievably disappointed. He was crushed. When you spend days, weeks, and months in anticipation of a single event, then that event collapses before your very eyes, part of you dies. "Christ, did I miss you. Then, half joking, he added, "If you want to be first, be at the fraternity house at seven-thirty. If you want to be second, be there at seven thirty-five."

"Don't talk that way," she answered scolding. "You know it's been a long time. We may have to start out slowly."

Not wanting to take any chances and screw things up he said, "I know. I'm sorry. I'll be good. I promise. See you there."

Slowly, Hell! he thought. *I want to rip her clothes off and spend the next hundred years lost in her flesh. But it ain't gonna happen. It just ain't gonna happen.*

Eddy thought back. What a candy-ass he was. The Montagnard chief would have hung his head in shame. He's the one who'd been to war. He's the one who had become a prisoner and was tortured. He's the one that fought for almost two years just to get back to her. His hurt turned to bitterness and fear. He started thinking the worst. Her only battle was deciding what dress to wear when she went out and *Jody-fucked* all his buddies while he was gone. He knew this probably wasn't the case, but a person's mind goes to the worst recesses of darkness when the feeling of rejection hovers over the soul. Especially since being with her was all he had been thinking about since the Montagnards found them in the jungle, one breath from the Grim Reaper's grasp, and he realized he was going to make it home.

That night at the frat house at seven-twenty, Eddy was standing on the porch in hopeful anticipation and up drove Marge. He was so horny he'd get hard if the wind blew. Some women just don't get it. It wasn't just the anticipation. It was also about a billion other little things that had occurred, building up during the entire time he'd been away, screaming to get out.

She got out of her car and started walking up to the house. Looking up, she finally recognized Eddy. Stopping dead in her tracks, she brought her hand up to her mouth as though she were stifling a scream. Her eyes were as round as pool balls. Instantly she shook her head *no*, turned on her heels, ran to the car and drove away. It was the last time he ever saw her.

Eddy was frozen in place unable to believe what he had just seen. All of a sudden he wasn't horny anymore. He was in shock. All of his fears had come to fruition. Rejection by a bunch of pot-head hippies was one thing. But to be rejected by the one reason he had held on to? The driving force *making* him take that *one more step*? Fight that *one more battle*? It was almost more than his mind could handle. He later found out through mutual friends that she thought he looked like a wild animal.

I was a wild animal, for Christ's sake, he thought in remembrance. *But I could have been tamed. Why couldn't she have taken the time? Was her love for me that weak?* He knew he didn't look like he did the last time they had seen each other. He tipped the scale at 128 pounds, had scars places most people don't have places, and looked like the poster child for Dachau.

At the party his fraternity brothers threw for him that night, he couldn't even get a girl to dance with him. And these were sorority girls he'd known before going to Nam. He finally got one to sit and talk, but only after he changed out of his uniform into civvies. As he sat watching everyone, except him, having a great time, his level of depression got greater and deeper. Even alcohol couldn't bring him out of his despair. He eventually just got up and quietly left.

Rejection, at this level is all encompassing. He couldn't seem to break out of it. It wasn't just his being rejected by Marge. That was bad enough. He was being rejected, and would continue to be as would most of his fellow vets, by the very symbol of hope he had held on to for so long. He didn't get laid for almost six months. He would have scored better in the Montagnard village than he could with his own ungrateful people.

Eddy remembered a couple of statistics that should make every American, who treated their returning *sons* as he was being treated, proud:

More American Viet Nam Veterans have committed *suicide* since coming home than were killed during the entire war.

Statistically speaking, over seventy-five percent of the returning Viet Nam Veterans are earning below poverty wages, and over half of them are *homeless*.

As he sat letting the rain have its way while his mind dove into the depths of depression, he questioned why no one cared. His fellow brothers in arms were homeless or dying because of that lack of caring.

Heroes were being made out of traitors. The most infamous example was Hanoi Jane. Jane Fonda, the bitch daughter of the famous actor Henry Fonda who spent the rest of his life ashamed of her, went to North Viet Nam in 1972 to see the POWs being kept at the *Hanoi Hilton*. She openly stated that, "If people truly understood Communism, everyone would want to be a communist." One time, a Col. Larry Carrigan was in the 47FW/DO (F-4E's). He spent 6 years in the *Hanoi Hilton*, the first three of which his family was only informed that he was *"missing in action."* His wife lived on faith that he was still alive. His group got the cleaned-up, fed and clothed routine in preparation for a *"peace delegation"* visit. They, however, had time and devised a plan to get word to the world that they were alive and still survived. Each man secreted a tiny piece of paper, with his Social Security Number on it, in the palm of his hand. When paraded before Ms. Fonda and a cameraman, she walked the line, shaking each man's hand and asking little encouraging snippets like: "Aren't you sorry you bombed babies?" and "Are you grateful for the humane treatment from your benevolent captors?" Believing this *HAD* to be an act, they each palmed her their sliver of paper.

She took them all without missing a beat. At the end of the line and once the camera stopped rolling, to the shocked disbelief of the POWs, she turned to the officer in charge and handed him all the little pieces of paper.

Three men died from the subsequent beatings. Colonel Carrigan was almost number four but he survived, which is the only reason we know of her actions that day.

In her eyes, the American soldiers were the aggressors and should have been treated accordingly.

She has never apologized for what she did. In fact, she has openly stated that what she did was the right thing to do and would do it again.

Eddy knew that she was a traitor to our country and the only Viet Nam Vet that doesn't hate her is John Kerry, another candy-ass backstabber who awarded himself medals.

Some hero. The 44th President wanted to nominate her to be named one of the top 100 women of the century. That idea did not go over very well with vets.

Hanoi Jane did more to hurt the way the veteran was treated once he got home than all the protesters combined. People in the entertainment industry should be very careful when voicing their opinions. Eddy knew that everyone had a right to their opinions. But people, for whatever reason, seem to hang on the opinions of movie stars like they were the voice of God. And he knew they weren't.

His hand hurt. He knew it was Psychosomatic, a sensation in the mind, not real, but he felt it nevertheless. It was as though it hurt for all those who could no longer hurt.

Back in the present, sitting in the rain thinking about all these hells he'd been subjected to, a dog walked up to Eddy and sat in front of him, staring. There was no viciousness in the animal. This rain-drenched Doberman just sat there, getting wetter and wetter, staring at Eddy and not moving.

"Get out of the rain, dummy," Eddy mentioned to the dog, knowing he couldn't understand. "Go on. Get home. You probably have a home and no good excuse to be out in this weather. Go on!"

The dog got to its feet, walked over to Eddy -- and licked his destroyed hand. Then he took a step back, looked at Eddy again, turned and walked away.

Eddy sat there watching the dog as it left.

"*Semper fidelis.* Always faithful," whispered Eddy understanding the true meaning of the Marine Corps slogan.

Then he stood up, wiped the rain from his face along with the tears that had welled up but were hidden by the raindrops, and started to walk back home to clean up for a job interview, another in a long line of futile attempts to find a place in his country. The attempts had been going on since coming home. He didn't know how much longer he could do it. The jungle was easier than this. He understood the jungle. He just couldn't bring himself to understand this.

He had almost lost all hope. People offered none. But this small act by the dog gave him the energy for one more try.

"Be proud, America!" he said sarcastically. "You treat your sons well! Animals treat us better!!!"

Chapter 2

HIS APARTMENT WAS A STUDIO, the one room style usually occupied by a guy out on his own for the first time. The bedroom, living room, and kitchen occupied the same room. A Murphy bed folded up into the wall, but he hadn't put it up in weeks.

Eddy kept the place clean and neat. No clothes on the floor. The bed, made. The dishes washed and put away. The furniture was dusted, and the bathroom scoured.

He didn't care about anything in the world, but he was a fanatic about his little apartment.

He'd seen the other side. In fact, he lived the other side. His first wife was a woman who didn't believe in keeping a clean house. Marrying her was a result of the rebound from the rejection of the one he fought to come home to. He wanted some kind of normality in his life. So, he married the first woman who said yes –- and for all the wrong reasons. Her idea of clean was one for the textbooks. He surmised that she either thought the place would clean itself, or if everything were left long enough, he would do it -- which, of course, he did.

It wasn't that he objected to putting in a ten to twelve hour day then having to come home and clean the house. Many single moms and dads do that every day. It was just that he wasn't single and his other half sat on her ass all day watching soap operas, drinking, and popping a muscle relaxer called Miltowns. She was a legal drug addict. Her whipped-by-life father, a really nice guy who used to be one of the foremost eye surgeons in the country, had been mentally beaten into submission and nothingness. If someone in the family asked for a prescription, he just wrote it out. His body and mind had stopped caring. He'd had five heart attacks and was forced to give up surgery, the one thing he loved. He became a school doctor, wiping snotty noses and putting Band-Aids on scratches.

Talk about demeaning!

Everyone loved him, except his family. They treated him like shit. His wife had long before stopped sleeping in the same room. Eddy witnessed, on one occasion, his wife slap her father in the face because he questioned the amount of pills she was taking. Her father usually stayed in a mindless state of inebriation. It wasn't with hard liquor. No, his addiction was to cheap white wine watered down and poured over ice in a coffee cup. He never ate dinner. He just sat all evening sipping on his cup. No one tried to help him. They wanted him that way.

Life eventually showed mercy. He finally died from another heart attack and was relieved of that family.

At first, Eddy spoke up about his treatment, but his wife told him to mind his own business.

This woman was a real jewel. Already having two children from a previous marriage she began at the ripe old age of fourteen, the only reason she married him was so he could support them without her having to work. The week after they started dating, she quit her job, which wasn't much anyway.

Once Eddy complained about the hours he was putting in and the type of work he did. At the time he worked as a route truck driver for Dolly Madison cakes. He had to get up at three in the morning to be at the depot, load up, and be on route before six. He never made it home before nine at night as he had a large route that covered an extensive area. His days off were Sundays and Wednesdays. If he wanted to go anywhere on his day off, he had to cut it short due to his having to get to bed so early.

The night before a day off, he was too tired to do anything. So, he never did anything fun. He had no release of any kind. When he complained, her response was, "You're place isn't to enjoy your job or your life. It's to support me and my kids and keep quiet about it."

The marriage ended when Eddy woke up one morning and realized she was trying to turn him into a slave like her father.

He usually didn't give a shit about anything. This fact was undoubtedly why the marriage lasted as long as it did. But, this one time, he did give a shit.

He left.

And when I say 'He left,' I mean *he left*. He told her he was leaving. She then responded by pulling a large butcher's knife and came at him with it, like the scene from Alfred Hitchcock's *Psycho*. He just stood his ground and let her come. When she got within his reach, he simply disarmed her. He had just a bit more training and experience in this field than she did. He didn't hit her or hurt her in any way.

After removing the knife from her grasp, he looked at her and calmly said, "You've got to be kidding me. Really? You pull a butcher's knife on me? I'm leaving. I'm responsible for my actions now, but if I stay I won't be. And someone might get hurt."

He turned and walked out the front door. There was a screen door outside the wooden one and when he went to hit the latch, he missed and the whole screen door came down falling into the front yard. He kept walking, scaled a ten-foot wall, got into his car and drove away. All this while she stood in the doorway screaming obscenities for God, the neighbors, and anyone else within the bursting radius of a small nuclear bomb, to hear.

He just didn't listen.

His other marriage was also an act of self-abuse. She actually might have loved him, but by that time it really didn't matter.

They say, *Love conquers all.* A very nice platitude, but not realistic. Eddy, before Nam, was always called the eternal optimist. Now people thought of him as a pessimist.

Eddy didn't agree.

Isaac Asimov said it best. "*A pessimist is simply a realist in the eyes of an optimist.*"

In Eddy's mind he knew that life sucked. People were lying, backstabbing, self-centered scum that would screw their fellow man for no other reason than they wanted to. And in doing so, could go to the furthest depths of depravity and perversion in accomplishing their goal.

This was not something he was told. He'd seen it with his own eyes. He dreamed it almost every night since he'd gotten back stateside. If he heard of someone doing something good, he saw that as an exception.

Even the IRS got in on the action. Another fact that is shameful: More Veterans are audited by the IRS than any other single group of people. Another show of gratitude from a grateful country. Eddy was audited, fined, and a lien put on everything he owned for something he didn't do. Nor did he understand. They showed up at his door one morning and took everything he had.

Instantly, he was homeless. He became like so many of his brothers and lived on the street. And, because he couldn't afford a tax attorney, there was no means of fighting it.

Eddy didn't want money. He wasn't looking for the easy road to wealth. He didn't want anything except to have the harassment stopped.

The IRS had levied his paychecks, seized his bank account, home, car, furniture, clothes, everything he had. His wife left him and immediately filed for protection under the Bankruptcy Act then for welfare. Bankruptcy won't stop the IRS, they go right through it, but welfare will. If the wife files for welfare, they ignore her and go after the husband for it all, especially if they are divorced.

Eddy refused to file for welfare. To him it was immoral. He had fought for his country so he wasn't going to suck off of it.

Declaring Bankruptcy was stupid. He didn't have anything left. What could he lose that he needed to protect? The IRS had it all.

He had to quit his job, meager as it was. Why work forty-eight hours a week as a warehouseman, another in a long string of meaningless jobs, breaking your back doing manual labor meant for someone twenty-five years younger than you, if what was left after the IRS took their share of your paycheck was under a hundred dollars every two weeks? Who can live on less than two hundred a month?

Did the IRS care? No.

So he didn't either. He quit.

The problem with this idea was he still had to eat. Homeless and rejected, he -- as was sadly the case with so many Viet Nam Veterans -- lived on the streets for a time. His bed would be a collapsed cardboard box in an alley placed under an overhang. He dined out, al fresco, every night. Most people don't keep their trashcans indoors. Friendship was plentiful. More than thirty of his fellow war veterans met on a regular basis at *The Club* to pass the time in conversation and camaraderie. The Club was what the homeless vets called the area of the park next to the dumpster by the pier. This particular dumpster always had half used bottles of wine and half eaten lunches left by the people who frequented the beach. All had a good time until the wine would eventually take its toll and the hapless individual would fall asleep under the stars.

On Christmas, Easter, and Thanksgiving, Eddy would find himself at the local mission, the only part of society that hadn't turned its back on the down and out. Sadly, the Salvation Army and other missions like them depend on the donations of others. When one gives to them, the giver is admitting there is a problem and society normally deals with problems by ignoring them. That way they don't exist.

But Eddy *did* exist.

Through all of this he was still a loyal American and believed in God and country. The holidays were especially tough. It was then that he sought the help and comfort of the Mission.

And it was through them, in an abstract almost surrealistic way, that he found himself involved in a lawsuit.

He had been on the streets for about five years. It was Christmas Eve and the thought of a nice warm turkey dinner with stuffing, candied yams, cranberries, green-bean casserole, and hot pumpkin pie, followed by the acceptable sermon -- the price paid for dinner -- then a warm bed with clean covers, worked its way through his abused brain cells. It was like a Pied Piper calling that anyone in Eddy's position was unable to say *No* to.

He actually enjoyed the sermons, a fact he would never admit to his friends except one.

Brother Timothy, the Captain of the Mission, never spoke down to the homeless. Eddy believed he really cared for those he had devoted his life to helping. A fellow war veteran, he understood their pain. Truly understood. He didn't just give *lip service* to his beliefs.

After the sermon, Brother Timothy would spend hours sitting and talking with the men and women who had gathered for the holiday celebration. It was during this time of friendly conversation that he learned of Eddy's plight.

Brother Timothy had known Eddy for years and knew he was a fellow Viet Nam Veteran, but until this night he was unaware of the circumstances leading to his condition.

Brother Timothy, it was said, was a loving man. But...did he have a temper? When he saw an injustice he made it his mission in life to right the wrong. He wouldn't stop. He was the most tenacious individual Eddy had ever seen.

That evening the sermon was on the value of friendship. How God put us all here together so we could help each other. No man is alone. No man can be defeated. No man can be a victim as long as he has friends. God was his *best* friend, but not his *only* friend. Jesus loved each and every one of his friends so much he always made sure there were others to help as well.

Friendship was a two-way street. If one receives a *gift,* true gratitude is not in words but in deeds. Help someone else. That is the way to say *thank you.* It may take years before you can. Or maybe it might be something minor like finding an extra blanket so you can be warm at night, then meeting someone with no blankets at all. Without hesitation or remorse you give him both of yours. You've had some warmth the last few nights. This person's had none. You can find another...and you do it with joy.

After the sermon, Eddy was sitting off to the side, sipping on a hot cup of coffee and talking with his one true friend, a fellow vet whose plight confused Eddy a bit. He seemed homeless but he never seemed as tired and drawn as everyone else...and he never smelled as dirty.

It was Miley. They had met the night before under a bridge trying to escape the rain. It was particularly cold and the rain was hard. Shelter was at a premium. This bridge, a drainage culvert running under a street, was the best he could find.

Ducking in, he saw that the luxurious apartment already had a tenant. Sitting next to a small fire he had built, from what Eddy never knew, was this man who looked up, smiled, and beckoned him to come over and share in the warmth. He introduced himself to Eddy.

"Cold night, isn't it?" the man said, more as a statement than a question. "We had rain like this in Nam but never cold. My name's Miley. Care for some soup? It's hot."

Eddy thanked him and accepted the gift. He wondered where he got the soup, but didn't let the unknown stand in the way of the welcomed sustenance.

At first Eddy thought he recognized the stranger, but on second thought probably not. As scrambled as his brain cells had become, he wasn't sure of anything. What if he had met him before? So what? The world of the homeless is a society of its own. To run across someone you'd met before was not all that unusual.

Sitting there, allowing the soup to bring warmth to his insides, he relaxed back against the wall. "I'm Eddy," he said feeling as though he had committed a social mistake by not introducing himself earlier. "Just because a person is homeless does not necessarily mean they're *mannerless*. Get it? *Manor-less? He was not to the manor born?*"

"I know," responded Miley. "We've met. And I remember your twisted sense of humor. It was another time. Another place. Good to see you again. Want some more soup?"

"Thanks," Eddy replied holding out his can. "You looked familiar but I wasn't sure."

"No special reason you should have remembered. Anyway, how have you been?"

"Not bad. And yourself?"

"Holding my own," said Miley in the typical response used almost as a code word between homeless vets. "Tomorrow's Christmas Eve, you going to the mission? They put out a pretty good spread."

"I know," said Eddy. "I go every year. Brother Timothy doesn't talk down to us like the lady at the other mission across town. He seems sincere."

"He is," stated Miley. "And he backs up what he says. He's a fellow vet, you know."

"That's right. I'd forgotten. But now that you reminded me, it does put a few things together. I'm glad he's there."

"So am I."

They sat quietly sipping on the soup for a few minutes, reflecting on private thoughts.

"He can help you, you know," stated Miley. "That is, if you want it. He won't push."

Eddy looked up. "Oh, I'm not so worried about my soul. By now I figure it's pretty much set on the path in the direction it's going to go. Whatever I get will be what I've earned. I stopped worrying about that years ago. I just don't want to be a hypocrite."

"Who's talking about hypocrisy and who mentioned anything about souls?" responded Miley. "I'm talking about getting you off the streets."

"What do you mean?" asked Eddy. "What could he do? Make me a missionary? Noooo thanks. I have a long-standing problem with them and I sure don't want to become one. He's the only good one I've ever known."

"No, no, no." Miley shook his head. "He has connections with people. If memory serves, you got it stuck to you by the IRS. Isn't that right?"

"Yeah. Good memory. I don't even remember you but you know my life story. (I've got to lay off of the sauce. It's gone way past shutting things out.)"

"He can get you through that too," Miley responded. "Why don't you ask him for help?"

"Who says I need help?" asked Eddy defensively.

"I'm sorry," came back Miley sarcastically, "but I didn't recognize you, Mr. Gates, in your Armani suit. Get off of it, Eddy. Please don't pull that ridiculously defensive posture so many of our down and out brothers pull to justify their misery."

"What misery?" asked Eddy. "I don't pay rent. I don't owe money. I have the world as my living room. I can eat the food from the garbage of the finest restaurants. The IRS never can destroy me again. I have friends and always meet new ones. What more could a guy ask for?"

Miley stared at him for a moment. "How about being able to hold your head up and be proud of the things you've done?"

"What do you mean?" asked Eddy. "What have I done so special?"

"Oh. Not much, I suppose," responded Miley slipping back into a sarcastic tone. "Of course there is your war record. I know it's pretty insignificant, but you are one of the highest decorated soldiers of the war. Doesn't that mean anything?"

"It used to, but not so much anymore," answered Eddy starting to get a bit miffed. Who was this guy, a comparative stranger, to come along and remind him of all of this? He had burned through many years and a lot of brain cells trying to forget. "I don't care about the medals. They can have them all back if they can take the memories with them. But to America on the other hand, it means even less. It means nothing. Why do you think we have so many brothers-in-arms who live as we do?"

"Thank you for making my point, Eddy. I'm sorry if I'm making you uncomfortable, but it angers me beyond words to see someone like you who has done so much and can offer even more throw his life in the toilet. Especially when there is an alternative."

"Thank you, Mr. Norman Vincent Peale, but your *Power of Positive Thinking* won't work here. Plus -- who appointed you the guardian of my life?"

"That's not important. Look, I'm just trying to suggest that you talk to Brother Timothy, that's all. I know you have all of this to lose," Miley indicated their surroundings and a dead rat that floated by in the small stream at the center of the culvert, "but we all have our burdens to bear."

"What about you?" Eddy asked in an attempt to change the subject off of himself. "Why haven't you gone to him? You're as bad off as I am."

Miley broke in immediately. "Thank you for at least admitting you are *bad off.* It's a start. But, we aren't talking about me right now. We are talking about you."

"Well, I don't *want* to talk about me anymore. I bore me. I want to talk about you. Why hasn't he helped you?"

"I'll explain later," Miley responded.

Eddy noticed he had a strange way of not answering questions he didn't want to answer. It was a little unnerving. He felt an unusual sense of trust and ease with Miley. He couldn't pin down why, but he did. Perhaps it was the brother vet thing.

"Why don't you settle back and get some sleep?" continued Miley. "Tomorrow we can go down to the Club and shower before going to the mission. Believe me! You could use one."

Picking up on the light tone of the last statement, Eddy reciprocated. "Oh? Excuuuuze me. I didn't realize I was offending your delicate senses.

Would you prefer, Sire, that I take my ill-gotten repose downwind of His Majesty so as to no longer be a detriment to his fragile nasal passages?"

"That's the Eddy I know," shouted Miley happily. His voice gave the impression that he had just won an Oscar or something. This guy was happy. His face was a grin from ear to ear.

Eddy stared at him. He just sat there grinning.

"OK," Eddy stated. Too many questions were popping up that were going unanswered. "What's going on here? Who the hell are you? How do you know so much about my goddamn life? Why are you posing as a homeless vet? You aren't homeless, are you? I have a gut feeling you're a vet but you're definitely not homeless. Oh! Now I remember! You're the son of a bitch that choreographed my enlistment and led me to become an officer. Thank you for that, by the way. But, why the push to get me to the mission? What the hell is going on?!"

"Yep. That's my Eddy, garbage mouth and all," stated Miley never losing that grin. "I wish the guys could be here right now. They'd love to see this. I could imagine what they'd say. 'You think he smells bad now. You should have gotten a whiff of him in country.'"

Eddy just sat staring at this guy.

."Goddamnit -- what are you talking about?"

"We really have to do something about your language," stated Miley.

"Who's 'We'?" asked Eddy about ready to go over the edge.

"Tell you later. Right now you should get some sleep."

"No! Right now you should answer my goddamn question. I'll get the sleep later."

"OK! OK!" stated Miley. "Stay awake all night for all I care. But I'm tired and tomorrow is going to be a long day, so I'm getting some shut-eye. You can do whatever you want. You always do."

With this last statement, Miley lay back down against the wall and pulled a blanket over himself. Within a heartbeat Eddy heard the deep breathing of a sound sleep coming from the pile of clothes and blanket.

While this was happening, he just sat there staring. Did he get any of his questions answered? He didn't think so, but maybe he did.

No. He was pretty sure he hadn't and this sleeping maniac wasn't going to satisfy his need to have a few million answers. He would have to wait until morning. Then...then, this guy would tell him everything he wanted. Once this new twist in his life was unraveled, he would talk to Brother Timothy.

Eddy admitted to himself he didn't like the way he lived. He'd never given up on anything in his life. He sure didn't quit when he was taken prisoner in Nam. And when he and his two buddies escaped with the help of a Russian Major, he didn't quit. Why had he this time?

Boy, he must have been heavily under the sauce when he talked to Miley before. He had no memory of telling anyone that much detail about his captivity.

And who was the IRS, anyway, that they could step in and destroy a life without justification or cause -- or even a *by your leave*? No organization has power unless people give it that power. No leader can lead unless people see him as such. But before anyone can see him in that light he has to see himself as one who can rise to the task.

When did he give up the fight? When did he conclude that he had the *right* to quit? This guy, Miley, had stirred up something inside of him that had been dormant for years. Miley was right. He had to get out of these conditions. The war wasn't over and never would be until people and organizations, like the IRS, recognize the sacrifices made by those who answered their country's call.

He -- this one lone individual -- could make a difference. All it takes is a few individuals to make up a group and a few *groups* to start a revolution. Not a bloody revolution but a change.

He couldn't make a change or anything in his present state.

Eddy looked down at his empty can that had held the soup. He wondered what kind of soup it had been. For the first time in over five years he was sober. Alcohol didn't cloud his thoughts. His mind was clear.

So was his destiny.

Chapter 3

THE TWO SAT TOGETHER AFTER the dinner and sermon talking. All day Eddy had been prying away at Miley trying to get some answers. Not a lot of success was achieved. Basically, he didn't know any more than he had last night.

Miley obviously was a vet since he was his recruiting sergeant. And he, without question, knew a lot about Eddy. He might, or might not, be homeless. He might, or might not, be sane. The guy kept referring to people as though Eddy should know them, and for the life of him he didn't.

He gave up trying to figure him out and just accepted the friendship. Finally it hit him. Not only was this the same guy that recruited him into the Army. This was the same guy that had plagued his mind so many times in the past. He couldn't believe it had taken so long to remember him.

How had he become homeless, if in fact he was? Miley wasn't Eddy's problem anyway. The IRS was. If Brother Timothy could help him, or if he knew someone who could, it would be a large step in the right direction. Doubt crept into his mind but it was worth a try.

As he made his rounds, Brother Timothy eventually found his way to Eddy and Miley.

"Welcome back my friends," he said in total sincerity. "I'm so happy to see you both. I didn't know you knew each other?"

"Yeah," answered Miley. "We met a long time ago but reunited last night. Shared a dry spot to get out of the rain."

"Good. Good. Did you enjoy the sermon? I admit I get a bit over-zealous at times but I just want what's best for you guys. If I was a millionaire, I'd build a big house and move you all in."

"If you were a millionaire, we'd move in. You needn't worry there," responded Miley laughing.

"Say, Brother Timothy," he began again. "Eddy here needs a little help. I told him you would be the place to start."

"Depends on what he needs help with," responded Brother Timothy. "Souls I can lead to salvation. The rest is up to you."

"It's not my soul, Brother Timothy," began Eddy. "It's my life. I don't like it very much. I've spent too long not fighting back. Defeated by a system that is supposed to take care of me, not destroy me."

"This is something I hear way too much. You're a vet, aren't you?"

"Yes."

"Viet Nam?"

"Yeah."

"Which unit? What year?"

"Fifth Special Forces. 1967 through 1969."

"You were there for TET, huh?"

"Sure was. Stationed just north of Kontum."

"See a lot of action?"

"My share."

"His share?" Miley broke in. "The guy ended up a POW. Why do you think he was in country so long? Because he liked the place?"

"Really?" reacted Tim. "Is that true?"

"Well, yes," answered Eddy then said very quickly, "but that isn't the help I need. That isn't my present enemy."

"I know, my brother," Tim sat down and placed his hand on Eddy's shoulder. "It's the booze. You can't shake the old monkey, can you?"

"No. No. For some off-the-wall reason I sobered up last night. I'm as straight as you are. It's not booze."

"Then what is it?"

Eddy looked at Miley who just sat there and smiled. He didn't nod, or nudge, or anything. Just smiled, like an idiot.

"What are you grinning at, you old spook?" asked Eddy of Miley. Then he turned back to Tim. "This guy knows a lot about me. Some things even I don't know. It's a bit unnerving."

"We'll talk about Miley another time. Right now, I want to talk about you."

"Are you going to pull that same thing?" asked Eddy about to give up and go back to drinking. "Every time I ask him a question, he always puts me off too."

"I'm not putting anyone off, Eddy," Tim commented trying to ease the situation. "All I'm attempting to do is find out how I can help you, and you're not telling me."

"Oh," responded Eddy, justifiably chastised. "It's the IRS. They ruined me. They took everything including my family. And it was all a mistake. None of it should have happened, but it did. They never even said they were sorry. I think I deserve better treatment from the country I fought to defend. Or rather, I did what they asked. I fulfilled my obligation then got destroyed for doing it. Isn't it amazing? The government spends millions taking young civilians turning them into soldiers, trained to fight and kill. But they don't spend a dime taking a trained killing machine turning them back into a civilian. I understand that just recently they started to hold classes for soldiers getting ready to be released from active duty. But who teaches the classes? Other soldiers. Why can't they get someone who is a civilian? Someone who knows how to be a civilian and operate in the civilian world? It's really no wonder there are so many homeless vets.

"It just isn't right! For the last five years I've sat back and taken it. Well, I'm not taking it any more. I want to fight, but I need help. Can you help me?"

Brother Timothy sat there in silence. How many times would he have to hear this same scenario?

Finally he said, "I can't help you."

His adrenaline working over-time, Eddy popped up on his feet. "Didn't think you could, but thanks anyway." He held out his hand to shake Brother Timothy's. Then he planned to walk away, find a cot, and go to sleep. He was tired. Tired of it all.

Tim stopped him. "I didn't say there wasn't help. I said *I* couldn't help you, but I know someone who can. He's a very successful attorney with an honest heart, a rare combination at best. I know he can help.

"I won't be able to get him tonight, or tomorrow, but you've waited five years. You can wait a couple of more days. In the meantime," he got up and slapped his legs, "get some sleep and stick around. Tomorrow we're going to have a great time with the kids and then another great dinner. The next day I'll call Al.

"Right now, I have some lost souls to save. Sure I can't save yours?"

"No, but thanks anyway. We'll stick around. We're much obliged."

"Don't mention it." Then Tim walked over to the next man as warm and helpful as when he came up to them. Eddy wondered if this guy ever ran out of energy.

He turned to Miley, "Ever hear of this attorney he's talking about?"

"No. Can't say I have. But if Brother Timothy trusts him, you can take that to the bank. I've never heard of him leading anyone down some path that had a dead end. I'll put money on the fact the guy's probably a fellow vet. Brother Timothy tends to keep us together, united in some way. It's as though he wants us to take care of one another."

Eddy thought about that for a moment. "Actually, that's not a bad idea. We few, who have seen the face of war, are the only ones we *can* trust. There is a bonding isn't there?"

"You bet there is."

"If I get out of this, if I'm able to fight my way back, I'll spend the rest of my life devoted to uniting that brotherhood. We're a bunch of individuals and separately we haven't been given thanks or respect. Have we?"

"No. We haven't. The evidence is all around us and on every street corner."

"United, however, we make up a formidable number. As a group we can ask -- no, we can *demand* that respect."

Miley sat back and watched. He got a kick out of Eddy when he was on a roll. And now, the old commander was back.

"No one," Eddy continued, "can expect others to respect them unless they first respect themselves."

"Do you respect yourself?" asked Miley.

"I obviously haven't been, but it's time I started." He reflected on this for a few seconds. "Yes. Yes, I do. I'm proud of the things I've done. Proud of my doing what I was raised to believe was right. Proud of standing for what I personally know is true. I'm even proud of the last five years."

"What?" asked Miley shocked at how anyone could be proud of being homeless, living off of garbage and sleeping in alleys. "How can you be proud of that?"

"Have I been a bad person?" responded Eddy. "Have I done evil things? Have I hurt anyone, or stolen from anyone? Have I not helped whomever I could? Who have I hurt?"

"Yourself," Miley stated.

"Yeah, well. Everyone's allowed to make a mistake. Making it isn't the sin. It's not recognizing that it's a mistake; you made it, so stop. Don't keep making it.

"I've stopped. I don't know what was in that soup you gave me yesterday but ever since I ate it a fire inside of me has been growing."

"It's called a *cup of human kindness*. I don't know what's in it, and if the truth were known I'm afraid to find out. But it does make you all warm on the inside, doesn't it?"

"That's an understatement," answered Eddy "Are you ever going to tell me who sent you to help me?"

Miley smiled, walked over to an empty cot, lay down and pulled the covers over himself. Just before going to sleep, he smiled and said, "Tell you later. Good night."

Eddy sat on the cot next to him and stared quietly at his slumbering friend. He wondered of there was a soup that would force Miley to answer one stupid question -- just one -- without putting him off.

Chapter 4

As I said, the lawsuit was successful and the IRS lost.

Eddy never got any of his property back, but he was no longer considered a vagabond and was employable. Hence his constant attempt at fitting back into a world that didn't want him or any vet like him.

Later, while visiting the VA Hospital where he had applied for some form of compensation, he was visited by a man from Langley. Exactly what the guy's roll was, Eddy never did find out. Because he had been Black Ops, they always kept a closer watch on the lives of the people who had worked for them. They never reached out and helped, but they insured that nothing subversive would take place. In other words, *they covered their own asses.*

Ironically, Eddy knew this guy. It was Miley... again. Eddy figured this was why he showed up and helped him find Brother Timothy. It wasn't a surprise, as he knew how he had been manipulated the whole time.

"So basically," began Miley. "You're telling me you'd rather be back in your jungle than here at home. Is that right?"

Eddy jumped in at that last remark. "It's not *my* jungle. I'd just as soon use the entire country as a nuclear testing site. When the bomb was dropped on Japan it was a tragic necessity, which has been argued for years. The damage was incredible.

"Drop a nuke on Viet Nam and you *might* do a hundred dollars damage. It's a worthless piece of real estate loved only by the thorn-rooted trees and deadly poisonous snakes."

"OK, OK," interjected Miley. "I get the idea that you don't like the place. I take back the term *your jungle!* Jesus, don't get so touchy. Has anyone ever told you why America was in Viet Nam in the first place?"

"Well, yeah," Eddy said, quite unsure of himself. He knew everyone was unsure. At least, every common man was unsure. They only knew what they had been told by their government.

"What was the reason?" Miley asked, testing.

"Well," began Eddy. "To stop the spread of Communism. To help the Vietnamese people from repression..."

"Bull," broke in Miley. "That's bull, and you know it. For God sakes, Eddy! You were a captain with the Fifth Special Forces Group, Special Operations, Black Ops, trained for assassination duty, and not paid by the Department of the Army. I don't know if you were aware of it but your pay came from the CIA budget."

"Yeah. I knew."

"OK, then. If you knew that, you should have known the real reason you were over there? Communism, my foot! Think about it. Do you believe those villagers, whose dialects were so different that two villages a kilometer apart could hardly understand one another, would care about political affiliations? Do you further accept the premise that the political atmosphere of a two-bit country three thousand kilometers from American soil presents any kind of a threat to the American way of life?

"Don't be an idiot. The rest of the country might have bought that cock and bull story, but don't let yourself get sucked in with the masses who prefer to behave like sheep. Don't let yourself be led around, blindly, by the nose. You're too smart for that!"

"Jesus!" Eddy reacted almost smiling at the intensity his friend had worked himself up to. "OK, Dad. I won't. Don't have a coronary on me. So what was the reason?"

"Magnesium!"

"What? Magnesium! What does that have to do with our presence in Southeast Asia?"

"I can see it is time for you to be educated as to the workings of politicians."

"Oh, goody!" Eddy said sarcastically. He hated politicians and he knew that Miley was about to give him more reasons to continue the feeling.

"Contrary to what most people believe, America's presence in Southeast Asia did not start during the Kennedy administration.

"I know that," stated Eddy. "Tell me something I don't know."

"OK, smartass. In 1941 Ho returned to Viet Nam covertly forming the Vietminh to fight both the Japanese and French. During the Second World War, China moved in and occupied the country.

"In 1946, China agreed to withdraw forces from Viet Nam. It was declared a *Free State* by the French. In May, France violated the agreement reached in March by proclaiming a separate government that was to be French-run.

"French warships bombarded Haiphong, November 23. Ho's Vietminh forces attacked French garrisons. The war was on.

"In 1950, a rising young senator from Texas took quite an interest in the country and its resources. He made it his life's work to get a piece of that action. Ho approached Truman and then later Eisenhower for assistance against the French. He was refused. France had been our Allies in WWII.

"1954. Viet Nam was split into two countries. The Texas Senator rallied behind Eisenhower to unite Republicans and Democrats to further the effort against Communism in the country.

"Now *this* was something Eisenhower could sink his teeth into. After all, the McCarthy hearings had taken place about this time and America was on a Twentieth Century Witch Hunt. Remember, Eisenhower was a general. He'd been the Commander of all Allied Forces in Europe during World War Two. Now when asked to get involved, only this time against Ho, he said, 'Sure! What's in it for us?'

"Please keep in mind that another struggle was going on during this period in history. It was a race, a race between America and the Soviet Union, the *Space Race.*

"Now, Eddy. What is a silver-white light malleable ductile metallic element that is found abundantly in Viet Nam, one that is used in metallurgical and chemical processes, the manufacture of pyrotechnics, and in construction in the form of light alloys, alloys especially suited for rocket construction?"

"Magnesium," Eddy replied listening to this entire revelation and being sickened by it.

"Right. Eisenhower traded U.S. help for magnesium. But, Eisenhower, being the general he was, decided to keep the whole thing secret from the American people. So he formed a group called *Special Forces* out of the best Ranger and Airborne units, which would train and advise. That was all they were to do.

"It was publicly declared that the American forces were in Southeast Asia to deal with the flood ravaging the Mekong Delta.

"The first leader of the South, Ngo Dinh Diem (1954), who was an ascetic Catholic steeped in Confucian tradition that even Ho Chi Minh respected as a person, was the one to approach Eisenhower through the Texas Senator. By this time, you should have surmised that the Senator was Johnson. Well, Johnson backed him, declaring he 'Knew of no one better.'

"May 1957, Eisenhower hailed him the *Miracle Man of Asia.*

"As it always does, time passed. Eisenhower's administration ended and Kennedy was elected.

"Now, Kennedy didn't believe in keeping anything secret from the people, so he revealed to the world the existence of this special unit and their function in Viet Nam. But, he was very adamant about the war being 'won or lost by the Vietnamese'.

"Kennedy got bullied around at the summit in Vienna by Premier Nikita Khrushchev, and he believed that America had a problem in making our power credible. Viet Nam was the place to achieve that goal.

"But, Kennedy differed with Diem in policy.

"After a few Americans got killed -- funny how that happens with all those bullets and rockets. Anyway, America was getting pretty unhappy with seeing a war on the Five O'clock News. It started getting hard to eat a TV dinner while a neighbor's son was being shot on TV and the South Vietnamese soldiers went home for the weekend. To them it was an eight-to-five, Monday through Friday war. Kennedy was ready to pull the troops out.

"Frustrated by Diem, Kennedy deferred the problem to Henry Cabot Lodge, the U.S. Ambassador in Saigon, who had Diem assassinated. This was not what President Kennedy wanted. He simply wanted Diem put on the right track.

"Kennedy was going to pull out after re-election in 1964.

"A few months after Diem's assassination, and Kennedy's announcement of the pullout...

"Bang! Bang! Bang! Three shots rang out in Dallas, Texas. Vice President Johnson is now President Johnson with full control over his pet project. Six months later, after the funeral and the country had its time of mourning, *POW!* In the Gulf of Tonkin, an American naval ship is attacked by a small landing craft from the north and Johnson declares the *Gulf of Tonkin Resolution* sending five hundred thousand troops to Southeast Asia. The war is on.

"A little known fact: To date there is not one physical piece of evidence that the Gulf of Tonkin Incident ever took place. But, war is good business, and if nothing else good can be said about Johnson, he was a good businessman. After all, his wife was a major stockholder in U.S. Steel, the leading importer of magnesium.

"Pop quiz, Eddy. How do you keep a war going so that the magnesium keeps flowing?

"HHOONNKKK! Wrong! The correct answer is: Don't call it a *war*. Call it something else. I know. Let's call it a *Police Action*. Nobody can get too upset over that, can they? Once something is declared a war, then you have to do really stupid things -- like *win it*.

"Well, once again, time passed. Johnson physically couldn't take the burden of this travesty once he was unable to hide behind others. He finally got what he wanted and his conscience took its toll on his body. It started killing him, so he didn't run for re-election.

Johnson is out. Nixon is in.

"A first rate politician and the ex-Vice President under Eisenhower, he let the *No Win* policy go on for a respectable time before escalating it to the hawk status for which he was known

"Then, all of a sudden, he, through some enlightenment of his soul and the pressure incited by Hanoi Jane and John Kerry, saw the futility of it all. Recognizing the public's unhappiness, which had only been going on since the Kennedy years, he decided to call it a day. He declared the embarrassing *Peace with Honor*.

"Little side-note, Eddy -- not that it had anything to do with Nixon's decision or anything -- but it was right about this time a synthetic was invented; Lighter, stronger, cheaper, and because it could be made in the laboratory, infinitely more available. It was named Kevlar. It even stops bullets when woven into a vest, and can be used to replace magnesium in spacecraft construction.

"So, we don't need magnesium any more.

"Bye, bye, Viet Nam.

"And, forget you: all the husbands, sons, and brothers that died or were maimed, both physically and mentally.

"Communism? Right!"

"Well," Eddy said with a huge exhalation of air. He almost felt as though he had been holding his breath the entire time Miley was speaking. "That certainly puts me in a better mood."

Sarcasm had become a normal tone whenever he spoke of Viet Nam, which wasn't very often. Why bother? No one cared. It was pretty much the same with most vets he'd encountered.

He continued. "Why not lay me down and shove bamboo under my finger nails? That would even be better. We got screwed when we got home. That was bad enough. But, now you're telling me we were screwed from the very start?"

He threw up his arms and turned around, taking a couple of steps away from Miley. It was a physical manifestation he did a lot, removing himself from the discomfort.

"What's the point? I mean, why bother with any of it? We're all a bunch of puppets being dangled on strings and the strings are controlled by insane egomaniacs who care about nothing and no one except their own power and the size of their purse."

"Why bother?" asked Miley. "Remember who and what you are. You're a vet. You have the protective instinct ingrained in your soul. You'll fight for others with no regard to your own personal safety or well-being.

"All change starts with the actions of one person. If you don't like the way things are, why don't you change them? There are a lot of veterans out there who would agree with you. Why don't you organize them and affect a change? It's better than sitting on your hands, moping about how bad you're being treated, and doing nothing."

"Pulling the *vet* thing on me again, are you? Look. A guy can only take so much. Sometimes it's better to cut your losses and walk away."

"I don't remember you walking away from your responsibility to Mal and Steve," stated Miley. "The odds were so stacked against you even Spock couldn't calculate the outcome. Yet, you didn't give up. You kept pushing and striving. You were not going to let Viet Nam get to you. You were coming home –- all three of you."

"You fight dirty, Miley," stated Eddy. "I hate it when you pull that stuff on me. Probably because down deep I know you're right. And I hate it when you're right all the time. What are you anyway? My wife?"

"Really?" responded Miley.

"OK. OK. Your right," admitted Eddy. "Why not? I'll do it. Happy dear? Since you came up with the idea, would you like to give me a helping hand? I could use someone I trust."

"Sure. Why not?"

Chapter 5

"So," began Eddy. "Where do we start?"

"Well, you probably want to set up a non-profit organization. Money is going to be changing hands, donations accepted, payments made, etc. You don't want to be taxed to death."

"Good idea. I never want to deal with the IRS again. I'll get a hold of Al today and find out what I have to do."

Eddy began.

He visited all the veteran's organizations to tell them about his new movement called *HELP ONE ANOTHER*, dedicated to veterans helping each other. Veterans come from every walk of life: Scientists, Teachers, Mechanics, Farmers, Ranchers, Carpenters, Cabinetmakers, Laborers, Retail Shop Clerks, Salesmen, Doctors, Business Professionals, Lawyers, Ministers, Law Enforcement, etc. Every talent could be called upon to lend a helping hand to their fellow veterans. Eddy was determined that no vet would ever feel alone or without hope again if he had anything to do with it. There would always be an organization that a vet could turn to that would help. And, no vet would ever have to pay for the services they received, whether it was medical, legal, or just having a car worked on. All costs would be absorbed by the organization.

He solicited donations from every source he could. Visiting all the civic organizations, churches, radio stations, and basically anywhere someone would listen, eventually the money started to flow in. Slowly at first, then much more rapidly as the word spread.

Sadly, most of the money came from vets. Non-vets simply wanted to forget about the war.

Well, Eddy wasn't about to forget about it. And as long as it was within his power, no one else would either, whether they wanted to or not. He would keep the plight of the veteran as ever-present in the eyes of the public as his hand was before his eyes.

The organization moved forward steadily. Miley was a great help and Eddy always showed his appreciation.

Restrictions and roadblocks were constantly thrown in their way by the government. They even went before congress to try to get legislation changed for more veteran's benefits. But, congress would always bury it. The Left wanted no reminder of the war, and the right didn't want to make waves.

After they had been going for about two years, they received a notice from the IRS. They were going to be audited. Eddy immediately contacted Al, who responded to the audit with a vengeance.

As it turned out the auditor was the same agent that tried to ruin Eddy's life before.

"The guy is a jerk," began Al. "He hasn't forgotten how we beat them before and he still holds a grudge. Evidently, losing that case, as they did, reflected poorly on the agent's record. When the opportunity came up to go after you again, even though it is your organization not you personally, he jumped on it. Plus, the IRS has a directive, not publically known, where veterans and their organizations are audited more than any other single group of people. They deny it, but it's a fact."

"OK," said Eddy. "Let them audit. We aren't doing anything illegal. They can audit until the cows come home, but it won't accomplish a thing. We are doing it right."

"That may be so," stated Al, "but I'm going with you to the audit. You aren't taking this on by yourself."

"I have no intention of taking it on alone. I have a CPA that's a vet who does our returns. He's going too."

"Good. Make sure you have all your records, and don't answer a single question unless I give you the go-ahead."

"We don't have to worry about that right now. The audit isn't for two months. More than enough time to prepare."

"Don't kid yourself," said Al. "Two months passes in a heartbeat."

"Don't I know it. Ok, thanks for helping. We'll touch bases at least once a week and go over everything. I want this done and over with quickly."

"It will be as quick as they will allow. I've known audits to go on for years. Settle yourself to the fact that this guy is out for blood. This is not going away quickly."

"OK," conceded Eddy. "I guess I'll just put it in your hands knowing you will do your best."

"On that, you have my word," promised Al.

Chapter 6

WHEN AL SAID THE IRS was out for blood, he meant it. The audit did not go well. Almost three years passed and the expenditures defending the non-profit status were financially and emotionally draining. Al never charged a dime, but the legal machine in the country was another matter. Plus, the time required away from running the organization taxed all those involved. Eddy couldn't do his fundraising, so the income suffered in a big way. The organization had an office, but they couldn't even make rent so they lost it. Nobody was getting paid.

Even though it was a non-profit organization, the personnel working still had to make a living. There is no such thing as an organization where everyone works for free. His employees started leaving, slowly at first. But eventually the only ones left were Eddy and Miley. He didn't blame them. He hadn't paid himself a dime in months.

When the results of the audit were finally released, the IRS declared that, in-fact, the organization was not non-profit and over ninety-percent of the deductions were disallowed. They owed the government over three million dollars, which they didn't have. A lien was placed on all the assets, including Eddy's car and home since he was personally signed for the entire organization.

Al appealed the decision, but the IRS was having no part of it. It went all the way to tax court. There were some successes, but not enough to matter.

The organization folded and Eddy lost everything. The IRS had finally gotten their way.

They never collected a dime, except for the assets they seized, but that didn't matter to them. Another vet was defeated. That was their only goal. This happened during the same time that the Tea Party went through their little problem with the Treasury Department.

Once again, the government of the country Eddy and others like him swore to defend, discarded their vets like so much flotsam and jetsam.

"Don't lose heart, Eddy," stated Al. "I'm not going to give up on this. *HELP ONE ANOTHER* did some real good, and if it's the last thing I do, I'm going to see that it gets reinstated and continues to do the good work you started."

"Thanks, Al, but not with me. I'm done. I can't go on anymore fighting other people's battles. There has to come a time when you say *enough*. Well that time is now.

"*Enough. Enough*," he continued quietly. "I'm through. I just want to spend the rest of my life living alone. I'll get another job. Pay my rent. Buy my food. And eventually die. If God wants me, he can take me. If not, it won't be the first disappointment I've ever had."

"I can make a few calls," stated Al. "I can get you a job."

"Thanks, Al. But, I can take it from here. You've done a lot. More, actually, than anyone could have asked. I appreciate it, but I'm done."

"Please let me help you, somehow."

"You already have in more ways than you can know. Thank you. But...yesterday was yesterday, and tomorrow is tomorrow. I have to stop confusing the two."

"In that case, have a great life, Eddy, and a lot of success. You deserve it."

With that, they shook hands and Eddy left Al's office. He went to sit at his favorite bench in the park. Something he had the habit of doing when things got bad and he had to think. And things were bad. He ripped the glove off of his hand and just stared at it. He'd picked up the habit of wearing a thin black glove over his mangled hand. It eliminated the stares from others and the subsequent explanations that would inevitably follow. But right then, he didn't give a damn about the stares from others or their opinion, for that matter.

His sense of defeat was all encompassing.

Chapter 7

BACK IN HIS APARTMENT, AFTER his drenching in the park in the present day and his encounter with the dog, Eddy stripped off his wet clothes and put them hanging over a rail in the bathroom to drip dry. He didn't want the other clothes in the hamper to get wet. He'd wash them all later.

Stepping out of the shower, he prepared himself for the job interview. Not owning a suit, unable to afford buying one let alone having it cleaned regularly, he put on a clean dress shirt and his one tie. He put on his glove and threw on a windbreaker then started out the door.

As he reached for the knob, his eyes caught some water on the tile floor that had dripped from when he came in from the rain. He went back into the bathroom, got a towel and wiped it up.

No sense having to come home and clean it, he thought. *It's always easier to do it right the first time than to have to do it over.*

Satisfied, he walked out the door. He didn't anticipate any better results today than the last dozen interviews he'd been on, but it was how he spent his days.

One interview stuck out in his mind and gave him a little chuckle. The Unemployment Office of the State of California had set him up with a job interview at a seafood distribution company. Eddy knew nothing about seafood, except how to eat it, nor did he know about distribution. But, a job was a job.

When he walked into the office of the owner of the company he saw a very large man sitting behind an equally large desk. The guy had to tip the scales at over four hundred pounds. He doubted the guy even knew the meaning of the word *exercise*.

After looking over Eddy's job application, this waste of humanity threw it down on his desk and looked up at Eddy.

"We don't have anything for you," he announced without asking Eddy a single question. "We don't need any *hired killers*."

Eddy calmly got out of his seat, walked up to the desk, leaned over until his face was a few inches from this fat pig's, and said in a soft, yet unmistakable, voice, "Be very grateful I don't do that anymore. If I did, you would be but a memory."

With that he grabbed up his application and turned to walk out the door.

The jackass behind the desk, after his heart receded from his throat back into his massive chest, which wasn't that much of a trip said, "That application is our property. You have to leave it."

Eddy turned to him and replied, "It contains my personal information. Therefore, in my opinion it is *my* property. It would, however, be fun to watch you try to take it from me. Just sit there like a good boy, put on some more calories, and watch your arteries harden. That is the closest you're ever going to get to doing anything productive in this world." Then he left.

Probably one reason he had a hard time getting or keeping work. Even though he lived with the feeling of defeat, he wasn't going to allow anyone to attack what he had done during the war.

His organization had had the goal of changing the way the country treated veterans. As stated, it had good momentum at first. But that fire lost its flame because of the audit and the government's many roadblocks. The Liberals still considered the veteran an embarrassment. The existing philosophy of the Left was: *The Viet Nam War was a hawkish moment in our history that was best forgotten.* Never mind the fact that it was a Democrat that got us into it to begin with. Historical facts have little to do with the opinions of the Left. They seem to twist history around to suit their own agenda at the cost of those who lived through it.

It was best if the veteran was cast aside and forgotten. A sad truth is that America has a very short memory. The Liberals know this and use it.

Eddy knew that whatever he was to accomplish, he would have to do it on his own. He would get no help from anyone. Brother Timothy helped him, as had Miley and Al. But that's where it stopped. The rest of his life was left in his hands and it was up to him.

He'd made up his mind that this job interview would not be like the others. He wouldn't allow his emotions to get involved. Little did he know of what lie ahead. His destiny was about to come to a focal point from which there would be no escape.

The rain had stopped, which always made for a better appearance. You know? Not wet! He could save a little money by not having to take public transportation, so he walked.

Chapter 8

HE SHOWED UP AT THE office where his interview was to be held typically early. He was always early to everything. Even picking up a date, he would arrive forty-five minutes ahead of time and sit down the street in his car reading. That was when he had a car. Eddy would rather wait than be late.

He didn't mind waiting. He'd done it all of his life. Why should now be any different? Sitting in the waiting room reading a magazine, not even announcing himself to the receptionist while passing the moments until the appointed time, he reflected on the company. The waiting room was on the top floor. Eddy figured that was where the executive suites were, so why not.

It was an insurance company, second only to IRS agents in ranking among the bottom-feeders of society. They set up a bet with you that there will be a catastrophe or you will die, depending on the type of policy. You're betting you *will* die. They are betting you *won't*. And, you're paying them for the privilege. Then, of course, after years and years of their collecting premiums and paying out no moneys except to the stockholders making them fat, if there is a loss, like in auto or earthquake coverage, they cancel your policy or find some way not to pay.

The size of the building was a perfect example of who won and who lost in these propositions. It was fifteen stories tall. All glass exterior and steel interior.

Eddy didn't like the morality of it, but a job was a job, and he needed one.

This interview was for a position in Claims -- that area where, after paying years of premiums then sustaining a loss, it is pointed out to the insured the fine print excluding that particular event, so there is no coverage.

Hence, no payment.

Is the insured's life ruined? Not really a concern of the company. But it's only reasonable to follow, because of the loss a trend is indicated so the policy is canceled. The insured can get coverage elsewhere. As it also follows, the elsewhere is more expensive and covers less.

Great Racket!

Anyway, this particular company was a sub-contracted claims company. An independently owned corporation dedicated to paying nothing. Obviously the company had made a lot of money over the years. The offices were beautiful. All the modern conveniences and technology was in place: Computers, full color copiers, holographic imaging and video conferencing. Every business convenience a company could want or ask for. The owner must be quite successful, not to mention rich.

When Eddy's appointment time arrived, he announced himself to the receptionist. Even though she knew he had been sitting there for the last forty-five minutes she asked him to have a seat. She would have someone right with him.

He laughed to himself and sat down. Again.

Ten minutes later, the receptionist informed Eddy that the personnel manager was out sick today and asked if he could reschedule for tomorrow.

"Not really," he said, not knowing why he said it. Because he was unemployed at the time, he didn't have any pressing engagements. He didn't want his emotions to rise to the surface, but it irritated him that he had made this trip for no reason. They could have called him at home and rescheduled.

However, that's *not* the way it happened! They waited until he had traveled all the way there. Then they waited the forty-five minutes until his appointment time watching him tick away his life clock. Continuing the lack of consideration, they further extended the delay for another ten minutes before telling him that he had wasted his time.

End of the rope. All emotions came screaming out. Eddy blew.

"No! I cannot reschedule for tomorrow. I cannot reschedule for next week, or next month, or even five minutes from now. I had an appointment for two o'clock, post meridian, today. I'm here. It's two ten. Where is my interviewer?"

"I'm sorry, sir. I've already told you that Mr. Trân is out sick. There is no one to conduct the job interview."

"Then build me one," stated Eddy with a calm force, implying that there would be no argument. "I gave this company the courtesy of being on time. They can give me the courtesy of meeting their obligation. Where is my interviewer?"

Just then, an Asian man in a suit stepped out from behind a partition. Before he said a word, he hauled off and slapped the receptionist across the face.

"I thought I told you to get rid of him," he said to the receptionist.

"I tried, sir," she responded in tears. "But, he won't leave. He insists on being interviewed."

"Your job is to do what you are told," he screamed. "Get rid of him! I don't care how, just do it!"

"Please don't fire me," pleaded the girl. "I have three children and no husband. I need this job. I'm sorry. I'll do better next time. I'll get rid of him. Just, please, don't fire me."

"Excuse me," broke in Eddy. "But I don't like being talked about in the third person when I'm standing right here. Plus, lighten up on the girl, will ya? She tried to 'get rid of me,' as you so rudely said. But I won't go. Hit her again and I'll rip your head off. If you want to pick on someone, try picking on me. That will be fun to watch. But lay off the girl." Then to the receptionist. "Sorry I caused all this. It's not your fault."

The Suit stood there speechless for a moment. When he finally found his voice he smugly said, "I suggest if you truly want the job, not just another *excuse* to continue your unemployment while living off of *my* tax dollars, you quietly make another appointment for tomorrow. And while you're at it, be grateful we're giving you another chance. Then take this opportunity to go out and buy a suit to wear for the interview. Of course, I still don't think they are going to hire you, but at least you will be presentable."

Now Eddy was pissed. "In the first place, if I had the money for the suit, I wouldn't need the job. Secondly, unemployment doesn't come from the tax dollars, but from the insurance you pay through the governmental withholdings from your checks when you do work. If you had the intelligence it takes to remove your head out of your ass, you'd know that. I'm here now. I don't want to come back tomorrow. I want my interview now! I don't give a damn if *you* do it. Just insure it's done."

"I have never been spoken to like that in my whole life!"

"Obviously," continued Eddy. "And equally obvious, is that it is about time someone did."

The *Suit* turned to Eddy and said, "Follow me."

So he did.

Eddy was certain this *guy* was showing him out the back way. But instead, he escorted him into a huge office that was more elaborate than anything he had ever seen in his life. The furniture was incredible. The paintings! There was Dali, Lassen, Goya, and Van Gogh, to name just a few, both classic and modern. The sculptures were of the finest artists. None of these were reproductions either. Eddy knew enough about fine art to tell the difference. All originals.

Shit! he thought. *That original Lassen costs at least five hundred thousand dollars, and that's being conservative.* He had seen many Lassen catalogues, but he had never seen this particular work. Yet, there was no doubt about it. It was a Lassen original.

Chapter 9

"I HAD IT COMMISSIONED," CAME the answer from behind, snapping him out of his trance of admiration.

It wasn't the strange voice suddenly heard that grabbed his attention. For the voice wasn't strange.

It wasn't the entrance of the man wearing the five thousand dollar suit that caused the instant shock to his system.

It wasn't the way this individual, carrying an air about him that declared his position and title, walked around to the other side of the desk and sat.

It wasn't the way his desk was built to deceive. The man was quite short, but seated behind the desk he seemed to anyone present very tall. He looked down on whoever was standing or sitting in front.

No. This didn't affect Eddy the way it should have. It didn't affect him, because an icicle had just been stabbed through his very heart and soul. Eddy knew, as he had never known before, that now he was lost. Lost in the fashion that only those having suffered beyond all limits of tolerance, and after being saved from that suffering only to be thrown back in time and time again, look up and ask *'Why?'* knowing there will be no reply.

"You treated Mr. Trân a bit harshly, wouldn't you say..." He looked down at Eddy's resume then back up again, "Mr. Chapman?"

"Eddy," he corrected vacantly.

"Well, Edward. Have a seat."

Eddy sat, more do to his knees buckling under him than because he was told to.

"Not the best way to act when trying to obtain a job. Wouldn't you agree?" the man behind the desk continued. "As you were told, today was not a convenient day for your interview. But since you feel that insults will get you further than simply doing what you are told, I will take time out of my schedule to conduct the interview."

Eddy just sat there. He hadn't heard a word that was said. His soul *had* died. He didn't move and didn't speak. He knew it wouldn't be necessary.

"Such actions are, of course, typical of your race and country. It is for this reason that we hire so very few of your type, only enough to satisfy the government and the *social do-gooders* who, screaming '*Political Correctness*' infest all enterprises looking for ways to stir the pot. The proper moneys can buy them off as well as they can a politician. Or didn't you know that? You native-born Americans are so ignorant.

"Do you know how I built this company?"

Eddy sat without a sound or movement.

"When I came to this country your government gave me, and all those like me, fifty thousand dollars cash and a house. I rented a small office and started my own business, fully subsidized by your government. My business was to help the fat capitalists keep their money by depriving the *deserving* people of it. They liked that. My company grew. The more I saved them, the greater the kickbacks to me. My company grew and grew. I incorporated, to protect myself and keep from having to pay my share of taxes, most of which only benefit the pathetic slime that walk the streets.

"Now, it is I who have the wealth. I'm the powerful one. Your people are so weak. You can pick on someone not in power, but where is your courage now? You sit there, wearing a glove on one hand. What is that for, anyway? Are you making some kind of a political statement? Am I supposed to feel sorry for you? Well, I've got a news flash. I don't. I don't feel sorry for you or your disgusting people. You will eventually lose your country to us, you know. Your weakness and greed will allow us to win. Not by war or terror, but simply by your selling it to us.

"It is almost humorous to think that you Americans gave us the money to do it.

"Do you know I still have the original fifty thousand? I never spent it. Never had to. Everything was handed to me.

"I'm originally from Viet Nam."

For the first time, Eddy spoke. "I know," he replied vacantly.

"You know?" responded the man behind the desk. "Good. Then you will take it as simply a continuance of the inevitable as I kick you out of this building, the way we kicked your entire military force out of my country. I'm only sorry there isn't some way I could get you to pay me for the privilege, the way America paid us." He sat back and laughed. "Actually it is all very humorous. Now! Get out!"

Eddy sat frozen for a moment then quietly got to his feet. He slowly walked to the door. As he weakly opened it, he turned to the man behind the desk and said very quietly, "Yes. I know who and what you are, Colonel Nguyên. But I can see you *don't* remember me. You can change your name all you want, as you obviously have. But I *know* you."

As he said this a surge of energy come over him. Where it came from, he didn't know. But, he had a strength and determination he hadn't felt since drinking Miley's soup. *When all is lost, you have nothing to lose.*

He walked back to the front of the desk and just stood there staring at this embodiment of Hell.

"Get out, I said."

"Oh, I'll leave," replied Eddy. "I'll gladly leave after you fully understand who you are talking to. You took everything away from me: My love, my drive, my country, my soul, my spirit, my friends, and my life. But I'm miraculously still here."

He walked around the desk and stood next to Nguyên. He then reached down and grabbed him by the necktie and pulled him to his feet.

"Take your hands off of me," shouted the Colonel.

Eddy let go of the tie, reached down and pulled off the glove. Holding his mangled hand up in front of the Colonel's face he asked, "Do you remember me now, you piece of shit? Do you remember what you did to me? Do you remember how you treated me? I do. I remember every word you spoke and every action you took.

"Calling you a piece of shit is actually an insult to shit. You are scum. You're not worth the time it takes to even threaten you. I will, however, give you a chance you never gave me. I'll let you call Langley and confess to who and what you are. I'll give you a chance to repent, as it were. If you don't, and right now, *I'll* report this to Langley and let them have their way with you.

"Say goodbye to your business, money, and life. It's over."

With that, he pushed him back into his overstuffed chair, turned and started to walk away.

The Colonel pulled open his desk drawer and drew a 45-caliber pistol out then pointed it at Eddy.

"You're not going to report anything, and I'm not going to lose anything. You think I'm afraid of you? No one knows who I was and they aren't going to. You're going to die right here and now. Why should I have remembered you? You were nothing. You still are nothing. Does one remember a pebble in their shoe? I do remember you now, however. I should have killed you in the camp, but that idiot Russian got in the way. Well, he's not here now and I have the legal right to protect myself."

He then shot Eddy twice. The first bullet passed through his body just below his shoulder. The second was a gut-shot that didn't exit.

After recoiling from the impacts, Eddy lunged for the Colonel before he had a chance to squeeze off another round. Grabbing him, he pulled the gun away and holding it against The Colonel's forehead he dragged him from behind his desk. The Colonel's eyes were as big as saucers. He couldn't believe Eddy was still alive.

"Are you afraid now, Colonel? I think you've been afraid your entire life. You're a coward. And you deserve a coward's death. But I'm not going to be the one to do it. I'll let others have that privilege. You aren't worth the price of a bullet."

With that he pushed the Colonel away. Unknown to Eddy or the Colonel, the bullet that passed through his shoulder penetrated the window behind the stumbling man, compromising the non-breakable, safety integrity of the glass. It was no longer non-breakable.

As the Colonel hit it, it shattered. Tripping on the edge, Colonel Nguyên plunged screaming the full height of the building impacting with the concrete pavement below. The screaming stopped.

Eddy stood, holding the revolver, staring down at the pool of blood that streamed from the dead body. He felt nothing. He didn't feel relief. He didn't feel joy. He just didn't feel.

He threw the pistol down and walked out of the office, down the elevator, through the lobby, and out the door into the street. He breathed for the first time. Even though he had won, he felt defeat.

Just defeat. Tired exhaustion. It was as though he had just at that moment in time, many years after the actual event, emerged from the jungle. Only to Eddy there was no more sanctuary. No village with loving caring people. No place to hide and heal. No home to go back to. Home was no longer home. Home is where you are welcomed, loved and appreciated. He saw now, that it hadn't been *home* for years. He just never wanted to admit it.

Well, now he admitted it.

Colonel Nguyên won -- and that was that.

Eddy walked slowly. There was no rush. His wounds hurt, and he bled. He needed to get help or he would die. Not from the shoulder wound, but from the gut-shot. He knew instinctively the bullet severed a major vessel. Death was eminent. But he didn't want help. He didn't want to be saved to continue his life of pain. To stay in this world that had turn so far against him and every other veteran. He just wanted to die.

Chapter 10

As HE WALKED DOWN THE street a car pulled up to the curb next to him and the door opened. A familiar face leaned over and beckoned him into the car.

Eddy got in without a second thought.

Miley asked him, "Where're you headed?" Then seeing his condition, "What happened?"

Eddy told him the whole story and asked Miley to drive him to La Jolla, if it wasn't too much trouble.

"La Jolla? Are you nuts? You need to get to a hospital."

"Please, Miley. I don't want to go to a hospital. If you have ever had any consideration for anyone, please do this for me. Just take me to La Jolla."

"Eddy...!"

"Miley, please. For all that's holy. Please, dear God, just do this one thing for me."

Miley stopped trying to reason with him. He put the car in gear and headed for La Jolla.

A little under an hour of silence later, Miley got off the freeway. Then at Eddy's direction, drove past the Scripps Institute of Oceanography and past the University of California in San Diego. He then turned left at the sign indicating the direction to Torrey Pines Hang Gliding and Flight Park. Parking the car he turned off the engine as Eddy got out and walked, in abject defeat, to the edge of the cliff overlooking the majestic Pacific Ocean.

Today, he would enjoy the view.

The wind was coming from behind him so no gliders were flying. In fact, the place was all but deserted. He sat down with his feet hanging over the edge. Miley joined him. He looked down the face of the cliff, three hundred and fifty feet straight down. No wonder the gliders got such a good ride from here when the wind blew correctly.

The sun was setting and the air was clean. He just sat watching the sunset over the water wondering, one last time, if he would hear the sound as the Sun touched the horizon.

He thought of Mal, Steve...and his country. He thought of Marge, the girl he'd fought to come home to. He thought of his brother and mother. He allowed his entire life to unfold before him like a movie on fast forward. As his life-blood slowly seeped out of his wounds, his life-force went with it.

"I'm cold," he finally said.

"It will pass," replied Miley who allowed Eddy his peace.

And it did. His vision went out of focus and eventually turned black.

Just before everything in this world left Eddy, one last vision flashed before his mind's eyes.

Oh. I have slipped the surly bonds of Earth
And danced the skies on laughter-silver wings.

The famous poem began, depicting greater than any other literary work the feeling of flight. The author was unknown, but the feeling it gives has sent many a person searching for that state of mind only a pilot can enjoy. Legend has it that during the Korean War a fighter pilot's plane was hit and he was plummeting to his death. Over the radio, as the officers and men in the command tower were listening to the battle in the sky, this poem was heard being spoken by one of the pilots. It wasn't determined who the pilot was until many years later, and that in itself has been left as a tribute to the ethereal nature of the piece. The poet was John Gillespie

Magee, Jr. It was titled *HIGH FLIGHT* and has been handed down, generation to generation.

Sunward I've climbed and joined the tumbling mirth
Of sun-split clouds -- and done a hundred things
You have not dreamed of -- wheeled and soared and
Swung high in the sunlit silence. Hovering there
I've chased the shouting wind along and flung
My eager craft through footless halls of air.
Up, up the long delirious burning blue
I've topped the wind-swept heights with easy grace,
Where never lark, or even eagle, flew;
And, while with silent, lifting mind I've trod
The high untrespassed sanctity of space,
Put out my hand, and touched the face of God.

If there was a God, Eddy was just about to *put out his hand, and touch Him.* Only it wasn't on *laughter-silver wings,* because his arms weren't airfoils and the human body has the glide path of an anvil.

Sic itur ad astra. Such is the way to the stars.

He slowly lowered his head and fell forward, plunging toward the abyss.

But he never felt the impact.

Death and Redemption

"Hello, Eddy. We've been waiting for you."

Steve and Mal were standing there, right in front of him. Eddy didn't know what to make of it at first. They were on a large grass plain that stretched to the horizon. A periodic tree was in place just to give the eye something to look at besides grass. It wasn't flat, but consisted of small hills that did away with any monotony to the view. A few streams wandered through the mounds. There was a single road that led to the horizon. The sky was clear and the brightest blue he had ever seen. An occasional cloud drifted by to give it contrast. Birds aimlessly circled in an occasional thermal that drifted past. The wind was light and the air fresh. The Sun was bright but not hot. The smell in the air Eddy couldn't place at first, but then it hit him. *Cotton Candy.* That wonderful treat mostly found at carnivals and county fairs, which brings to the forefront of one's memories all that was good and fun in their youth. It was perhaps the most perfect day he had ever seen.

"Where am I?" asked Eddy. "Is this a hallucination, or is it real?"

"Oh, it's real," said a fourth voice from behind him.

Eddy turned around to see Miley standing there with a smile on his face.

"This is Heaven, Eddy. You died and I brought you here."

"You brought me? What do you mean, 'You brought me?' How did you bring me? Are you dead, too?"

"No. I'm an angel."

"A what?!" asked Eddy.

"An angel," answered Miley. "Just like Mal and Steve are."

He turned around to look at his two old brothers in arms. "You guys are angels?"

"Boy," started Mal. "He doesn't miss a trick, does he?"

"How did you become angels? Have you always been angels? What in your sick lives did you do to cause you to ever be eligible to qualify to be angels? I can kind of see how the Preacher's kid could do it, but really?"

"He may not miss a trick, but he's just as sarcastic as ever," commented Steve.

"How do I know I'm in Heaven? Where are the streets of gold? Where are the alabaster cities? Where are your fellow angels flying around singing *Hallelujah*? How do I know this isn't some trick my mind is playing on itself?"

"Eddy," broke in Mal. "You died. You remember doing that, don't you? Colonel Nguyên fell out the window after shooting you then I picked you up taking you to Torrey Pines. We sat watching the sunset as your life on Earth slowly left you. The last thing you remember was *HIGH FLIGHT*."

"How would you know that?" asked Eddy.

"I'm an angel," replied Miley. "The sooner you accept it, the easier this is going to be. Look at your hand."

Eddy looked down at the mangled mass that he had come to know so well and hated so much. Only, now it wasn't mangled. It was whole and normal. He reached up and touched his head. He had hair. It was then that he looked at Steve and Mal. It hadn't registered at first, but they were the same age as when they were in country together.

"How old am I now?"

"Age is inconsequential," replied Miley. "We perceive each other as we remember them. We see everything as we want to see it. Here is true peace. Time has no meaning. We never get old or sick. All of the problems we had on earth are gone. This is a different existence. A different reality."

"How did I rate? I did a lot of wrong things in my life. I never really believed in Heaven or God. What did I do that allowed me to be brought here?"

"You always believed in God, Eddy," replied Miley. "Your belief was manifested in your heart and deeds, not your words. Too many people walk around talking about being good, but never doing anything about it. You did. You're a vet, for God's sake. *Every* pun intended.

"Let's take a walk."

They all started down the path toward the horizon.

"I have a million questions to ask," began Eddy.

"Fire away," replied Miley.

"Do I have to stand before God and be judged for my wrong doings? If he finds me bad enough, do I get sent to Hell? If you are an angel, where are your wings? How long have you been an angel? You always seemed to be around. Were you sent to watch over me, or something? Is God kind, or vengeful? Where is Colonel Nguyên?"

"The last question, I can answer," broke in Mal. "He didn't make it this far. In fact, he never made it into the *Book of Life* for consideration. He was judged a long time ago."

"OK," said Eddy, not sure how to feel. "What about my other questions?"

Miley began. "Eddy, God doesn't hold court as on earth. Judgment is loving, immediate, and final. There is no arguing about it. Your goodness far outweighed any wrong you did. You are most definitely *NOT* going to Hell. I have my wings. You're just not looking for them. Artists who have depicted angles as being a cross between men and birds missed the whole point of Heaven and not being bound by the laws that apply to the Earth. We don't need something to break the law of gravity then ride the air causing us to be propelled from one place to another. It's immediate. If we are to be somewhere, we're there. Right then. We don't fly from one place to another. We simply are there. Time and space don't apply in Heaven. A day here is a million years on Earth. The orbit of the Earth around the Sun, or the rotation of the Earth around its axis does not calculate our time.

"Think about it. What was a day to us before the Universe, Milky Way solar system, and Earth were formed? How do you think God made the Earth in six days? Our days are a bit longer. There is no time here. All time is now.

"As to how long I've been an angel? Well, let's just say I was one of the chosen that told Abraham he didn't have to sacrifice his son Isaac, told Mary she was going to have a child, broke the news to Joseph, and led the Three Magi to follow the Star.

"Yes, I was sent to watch over you."

"Well," broke in Eddy. "You didn't do a very good job. I went through a lot of hell."

"You had to," said Miley. "Where is it written that anyone is guaranteed an easy life?"

"Easy? I'm not talking about *easy*. I'm talking about my life. If you've been watching over me you know what I've been through. You know what Mal, Steve, and I went through."

"Yes, I do," interjected Miley. "And why did you do it all? You always had a choice. We take very seriously the concept of *Free Will*."

"I didn't have *Free Will*. I didn't have a choice. I was thrown into every experience I had. It wasn't by my choosing."

"Really, Eddy," said Miley. "Let's take a look at a few of the *'I didn't have a choice in the matter.'* Shall we?

"When you had the side of your face opened up by Dylan in high school, whose idea was it to flip him off?"

"He flipped me off first."

"But, who decided to bring themselves down to his level and return the gesture?"

"Well, me. I suppose."

"Suppose, Eddy?"

"OK. It was me. Happy?"

"Let's continue. Who made the choice to join the fraternity and party their way from eighteen units down to four making you eligible for the draft?"

"Boy. You really do know me, don't you? Why didn't you stop me from doing it?"

"Free Will. To continue: Who caused you to choose Multi-engine Airplane Repair?"

"Me."

"Who made the choice to go to OCS?"

"Me."

"Who made the choice to get a commission in the Artillery?"

"Me."

"Who chose to go on to Ranger, Airborne, Special Forces, and Black Ops?"

"OK. OK. I get it."

"Who made the decision to volunteer for Viet Nam so his brother could come home from Korea?"

"I said, OK! It was me."

"Who came up with the idea of burying themselves in the ground for days to thwart the attack on the Korean Battery during TET?"

"Me," answered Eddy, again hanging his head like a little boy who got caught with his hand in the cookie jar.

"Who made the choice to accept the assignment to take out the Colonel?"

"Now, wait a minute there. I was given orders."

"And you always had the choice to decline an assignment. That was part of the deal. Right?"

"I suppose."

"Who decided to stop the pain of your friend being skinned alive?"

"Me."

"Who decided to escape while you were being taken north?"

Eddy did a big exhale. "Me."

"Who finally turned to God in prayer your last night in the jungle?"

"Me."

"Who got rid of that poor example of a *Man of God* in the village?"

"Me."

"Who started *HELP ONE ANOTHER*?"

"Now wait right there. You talked me into that."

"No. I gave you the idea. I didn't talk you into anything. Whose choice was it?"

"Mine."

"Who came to the defense of the receptionist at the claims company owned by Nguyên?"

"Me."

"Who chose to give Nguyên a chance to redeem himself before you turned him in to Langley...?"

"Me."

"...which was taken as a threat causing him to pull the 45 and shoot you?"

"I said you made your point," yelled Eddy. "It was me. OK! It was all me. I admit it. OK! Ultimately we all make our own choices."

"Thank you," responded Miley quietly. "Now Eddy. I only have one more question."

"Oh. Please continue," said Eddy sarcastically. "You're on a roll and I wouldn't want to spoil your fun. Go for it. What's the question? I'm peeing in my pants."

"Cute. The question is a rather simple one."

"I'm waiting."

"Why," began Miley, "did you make those choices?"

Eddy stood there looking at Miley. He switched his vision to Mal, and then to Steve, who were standing there with grins on their faces not saying a word.

"Why?" repeated Eddy.

"Yes. Why?" said Miley. "Take a moment and think before you answer."

"I honestly don't know," replied Eddy. "I suppose there were a lot of reasons. I can't think of any one reason."

"Yes, you can. What was the deep down, ultimate motivation for you to have made the choices in your life that you have?"

"Well. I suppose, if I'm to be totally honest..."

"I suggest you are," interjected Mal.

Eddy stared at him for a moment then turned back to Miley. "When I was a child, I did most things for myself."

"And when you became an adult?" asked Miley.

"Ultimately I thought I was helping others, individually or collectively."

"Thank you, my friend. Thank you. That is the realization you had to come to before we could go forward."

"Go forward to what? What are you going to do to me now?"

"Eddy? What do you think is the ultimate mission of a soldier and a veteran?"

"To help those who can't help themselves. To fight for what is right. To stand between those who would conquer and control, and those who would be controlled. To be willing to give the ultimate sacrifice for another."

"What do you think is the ultimate mission of an angel?"

"Now *that* is a question I would have no idea of the answer," responded Eddy.

"It's the same, Eddy. It's the same.

"Where do you think we get our angels?"

"I always thought God created them," answered Eddy.

"Ultimately he did. He created the original ones. But as time has gone on, we've needed more and more. Where do they come from?"

"God creates them, too?"

"He does create them, but not originally as angels. He creates them as man and they have to earn their wings."

"Here we go with the wings, again. I don't see any wings on you three."

"I don't see any on you either. But did you not earn your wings in Jump School? Does a pilot not earn their wings after completing Flight School?"

"Yes."

"We choose our angels from the veterans that have demonstrated an unending desire to champion and help others. That is their Jump School. That is their Flight School. America may not have shown its gratitude and appreciation for what a veteran does, but don't think that God shares that line of thinking."

"What are you saying?" asked Eddy quietly.

"I'm saying, Eddy, that you are now, and will be for all eternity, an angel. Congratulations. You earned it."

With that, Miley shook Eddy's hand, as did Mal and Steve. All had big grins on their faces, except Eddy, who stood there speechless.

"I'm an angel?" he finally said.

"Yep," replied Miley. "Now the work begins."

"What work?"

"We have to watch over man. Let's go."

"Where are we going?" asked Eddy.

"We're going HOME."

And they continued walking

Postscript

IN WRITING THIS WORK MY sole purpose was to bring to the forefront the true tragedy of the Vietnam War: The treatment of the returning veteran.

I'm happy to say we have made great strides to correct that fault. But, It isn't enough and we can never allow it to happen again.

I further attempted to decry a warning.

Listen to your veterans. They alone have the experiences tempered by war to advise and lead.

In reading this story you may notice an omission. So that you don't believe it was simply a case of poor writing, let me explain why I chose this technique.

The omission I am referring to is the description of the personage of Eddy. I wanted each reader to picture him in *his or her* way. If a character is not described in detail, a reader will usually fill in that gap by personifications they are use to: Color of skin, eyes, hair, height, and body structure. These, I wanted each reader to personalize, to see through their mind's eye.

Veterans come in all colors, shapes, and sizes. I wanted Eddy to be every one of them: A favorite uncle, brother, son, husband, father, grandfather

Eddy belongs to America. We created him.

Now, we should --

TAKE CARE OF ONE ANOTHER.

During the writing of this work, I saw the film produced and directed by Steven Spielberg, *Saving Private Ryan*. This shows how long it took me to finalize the book. To date this film is the most accurate depiction of war ever put before the movie going public. It made the same statement I have attempted but I'm sorry to say, was put in the wrong hands.

I'm not implying that the film was anything less than incredible. I was moved beyond words. It left me speechless. Spielberg is, unquestionably, if not the best then one of the best filmmakers of our time. However, he is not a vet. His father is, not the son.

Because of this lack of experience and the accompanying perspective, all he could do was go by his military advisors, none of which were his equal in telling a story.

The film was incredible, well made, well acted, a definite front-runner for the Academy Award and should have been the winner.

However...in my humble opinion, his lack of personal experience allowed him to make one small error that could have taken it from being a great film and put it into the realm of the immortal.

Who was Private Ryan?

I'm not referring to the personage of the character, but rather what he stood for -- symbolically.

When the Captain told him to "earn this," referring to the sacrifice all the men had made, what did he mean?

The simple minded, never having stared down the *'Dogs of War,'* would say he meant to make something of his life as an individual.

But I'm afraid that is too easy. That answer lets us all off the hook far too fast. It allows Americans to continue in their everyday life shaking their heads at war. -- Bad! Bad! -- While we all, yet again, continue unaccountable.

Life, history, fate, God, whatever term you choose, won't let it happen.

I ask again. Who was Private Ryan?

I submit, and would have the agreement of every combat veteran in the world, Private Ryan was *ALL* of our Brothers-in-arms, and all of our countrymen who stayed home. He stands for that spirit or entity we fought and died for.

To make my point, allow me to paraphrase the script:

If the soldiers stayed at the bridge, putting their lives on the line, fighting, dying...? If they did that to save (instead of Private Ryan, substitute their fellow soldiers and country), then they would have all earned the right to go home to a *grateful* country. And that same country would be grateful because it fully *realized* the sacrifice.

What is the mission of a soldier and the heart of the veteran except this self-same act?

At the end of the film as Ryan, now an older man, is looking down the rows and rows of crosses and stars of David at Arlington National Cemetery almost countless in number and remembering those sacrifices, turns to his wife and asks, "Am I all right? Am I a good person? Did I *earn* these sacrifices?" Which one of us, alive today and breathing the fresh air of freedom, can truthfully answer that question in the affirmative?

Have we as veterans stopped fighting for what is right? Have we as citizens of the greatest country on this planet lived the kind of life that would reflect gratitude to those who sacrificed? Have we as a country lived honoring those sacrifices and those who sacrificed? Have we required -- no —- demanded that our politicians be accountable and grateful.

Spielberg's error was when the question was asked the wife turned, looked at him and said, "Yes. You're a good man."

Mr. Spielberg, I'm sorry but the answer is not "Yes".

It would have been far more profound if she hadn't answered. We *haven't* lived up to the sacrifice and we *don't* properly honor those who gave their all.

Until we do, the answer can only be ....
....
.........silence.

Viet Nam 1968

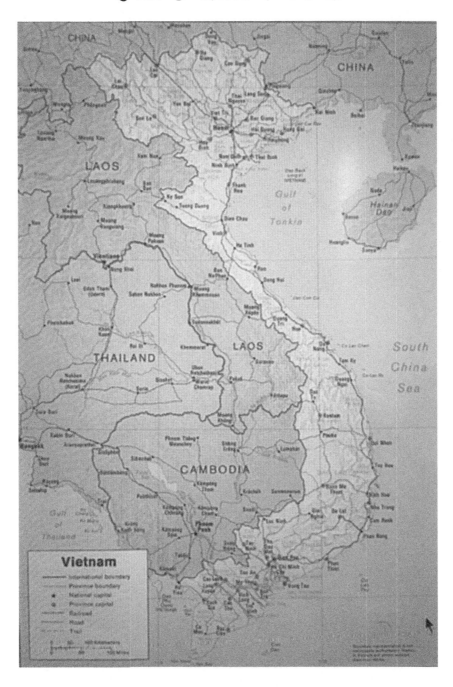

The Escape Route

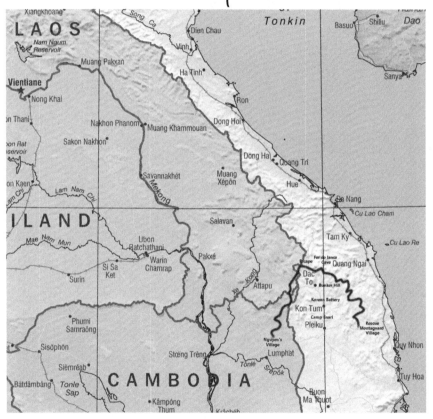

THE AUTHOR IN COUNTRY

About the Author

WALT DODGE IS A HIGHLY decorated veteran of theVietnam War. He later became a certified teacher in California holding three credentials, an actor and director on stage and screen, plus a musician and composer winning the Drama Critic's Circle award for best original score for Shakespeare's Tempest performed at the Globe Theatre. He has worked in Timeshare for thirty years where he is considered one of the best in the industry. Dodge was included in the 1984 edition of Distinguished Young Men of America. His previously published works include the novels The Nicoli Conspiracy and How to Survive a Hawaiian Honeymoon published by AuthorHouse. Also the novellas Time Soaring, The Competition, and Curtain Time. He lives in Southern California with his wife, children, grandchildren, great-grandchildren, and dog, Shylo.